'Then we have two
people the truth—and there's nothing so ────
that—people split up all the time. Or we stay and don't
tell anyone anything.'

His first alternative was quite unthinkable. She could
not stay and work here, among all these people who were
still strangers, and have them knowing. . .talking.

'You mean. . .pretend. . .to be strangers?'

'Something like that.'

'Do you mind?'

'If you mean, do I mind acting a part. . .' Michael
shrugged as though it was no big deal. 'If you mean, do
I mind what's happening. . .I'm not sure. That's what I
came up here to sort out. I'm beginning to think it might
just have been the best thing that could have happened.'

Alex gave a small anguished sound which she quickly
stifled. He seemed not to have heard but said lightly,
'Now, I suggest we return to the party, before people
begin to read a budding romance into this tête-à-tête in
the moonlight.'

He looked down at her with a lopsided grin, then his
face hardened and his hand went out and grasped her
arm tightly.

'But first,' he said, 'I think we have some unfinished
business.'

For Judith Hunte, writing Medical Romances is a happy merging of two major interests, nursing and writing. Judith worked for several years as a librarian before beginning nursing training, eventually qualifying as a registered nurse and midwife. She left nursing to marry and have her family, a son and two daughters, then returned to work in various Australian hospitals for several years.

Early retirement has given her the opportunity to indulge a lifelong yen to write. Her own nursing experience provides the background for her stories.

Previous Title

THE HEALING OF DR TRAVIS

ENTER DR JONES

BY

JUDITH HUNTE

MILLS & BOON LIMITED
ETON HOUSE   18–24 PARADISE ROAD
RICHMOND   SURREY   TW9 1SR

*First published in Great Britain 1991
by Mills & Boon Limited*

© Judith Hunte 1991

*Australian copyright 1991
Philippine copyright 1991
This edition 1991*

ISBN 0 263 77111 3

*Set in 10 on 11½ pt Linotron Plantin
03-9101-54950
Typeset in Great Britain by Centracet, Cambridge
Made and printed in Great Britain*

CHAPTER ONE

DR DOUG WESTON couldn't believe his luck!

He was one of the hosts at tonight's shindig, and he felt he had already rendered service beyond the call of duty. The party, a dinner-dance, was being given for the staff of the new Mackay Community Hospital by the consortium of doctors whose brainchild the hospital was.

The guests were a pretty mixed bunch, thought Doug. Those two middle-aged nurses he'd just been entertaining—battleaxes, he privately termed them. He'd been charming to them for a good five minutes. Then, with what he considered a stroke of genius, he'd introduced them to an elderly local couple who, he knew, had an interesting collection of medical problems they were always ready to talk about. In no time the four of them were hard at it, discussing symptoms, and Doug left them to it with a sigh of relief.

Now he was casting an eye around for more promising company. And virtue was rewarded!

Hesitating just inside the door was as stunning a female as he had seen in a long time—slim, with black hair, large blue-grey eyes and a perfect complexion. Her enchanting mouth lifted at the corners in a tiny smile. Doug liked that smile. He could tell that here was someone who was looking for a good time tonight. He was more than happy to do whatever he could to help her achieve that end. Quickly, in case someone beat him to it, he elbowed his way through the crush to her side.

Alex McLachlan, arriving when the party was in full

swing, was thinking happily to herself that she had not, after all, quite lost the capacity to enjoy herself. She had almost forgotten, in the last three months, what *joie de vivre* felt like, so it was reassuring to feel the lift of her spirits in response to the glitzy party scene and the medley of voices, laughter and music.

She smiled happily at the very young-looking doctor who was introducing himself as one of her hosts for tonight. She accepted the drink he found for her and allowed herself to be led further into the already crowded room—the reception-room of the town's most upmarket resort hotel.

Doug Weston's conversation, she soon discovered, consisted mostly of questions. Where had she trained? Did she have friends in Mackay? Family in Sydney? Why had she come here to work? She saw him surreptitiously glancing at her left hand and suspected that the one thing he really wanted to know was whether she was as unattached as she appeared to be.

In the past week, during which she had been working at setting up the theatre unit in the new hospital, prior to the opening of the hospital in two days' time, she had had plenty of practice at answering questions in a way that satisfied the enquirer, while revealing nothing about herself she didn't wish to reveal. She told Doug Weston she had seen an advertisement for staff for the hospital in a medical journal. She was a keen sailor, and Mackay, situated on Queensland's northern coastline, was the gateway to the Great Barrier Reef and the Whitsunday Islands and offered marvellous scope for sailing.

She did not tell him that it also seemed an ideal place for someone who wanted to put distance—a lot of distance—between herself and Sydney. Or that her one dread during the past week had been that someone who had known her in what she now thought of as her 'past life' might also have been appointed to the staff of the hospital. But that hadn't happened and, with staff quotas now complete, she could breathe freely.

Ten minutes later, Doug Weston was still firmly by her side and showing no inclination to go about his hostly duties elsewhere. Or even to introduce her to anyone else. Alex was eager to meet people. The snippets of medical talk that reached her ears from groups nearby were tantalising. Her nursing career had been in limbo for three months, and it was like water to a thirsty soul to be part of a medical fraternity once again. She decided she would wait for a few more minutes, then suggest to Doug that they mingle.

She said, 'If noise level means anything, your party is going to be a huge success.' Then, because she had been thinking along those lines, she added, 'It will be interesting, won't it, to see how we all shake down together?' Immediately she knew that had been an unfortunate remark which would meet with a predictable response.

Sure enough, Doug's eyes brightened and he grinned. 'Or who shakes down with whom!'

Alex bit back the squelch that rose to her lips and merely said, 'That too, I guess,' adding, 'Please don't let me keep you any longer from your duties. There must be others. . .'

Her hint fell on deaf ears. 'No problem!' he said cheerfully. 'I guess everyone's here by now. Although I don't see. . . Oh, yes, there he is, just arriving!'

Alex followed the direction of his eyes. She and Doug Weston were now well down the length of the room and she had difficulty seeing the door through the crush of people between. Then the crowd moved and she could see more clearly. Whoever the newcomers were, they must be of some importance, judging by the reception they were being afforded by guests nearby. She could see a distinguished-looking man with silver hair, laughing and responding to greetings. She saw him turn and draw forward whoever it was with him. As the second man came within her view, Alex gave an involuntary gasp. For one long, shocked moment her heart seemed to stand still, and then her blood was pounding in her ears.

It couldn't be! It was not possible!

But, even while she was telling herself that it was just one of those remarkable resemblances that did sometimes happen—that it was not really him at all—her racing pulse and the tight, suffocating feeling in her throat were putting the lie to that theory.

Nobody else could possibly have just that combination of strong, chiselled features and determined jawline, offset by a mobile mouth and roguish dark brown eyes. She watched, mesmerised, and saw his left eyebrow shoot upwards in response to something someone had just said. He replied, and there was a shout of laughter from the group around him. That confirmed it—if confirmation were needed—the eyebrow and the laughter. Wherever Michael Jones was, there was bound to be laughter.

But there was no laughter in Alex as she continued to watch—only a despairing incredulity that fate should have played such a dirty trick on her.

Inevitably, as though compelled by her gaze, Michael Jones looked up and saw her. The smile remained on his face, but it became fixed and, even at the distance that separated them, she could see that there was no laughter in the eyes that held hers for a moment that seemed to last for eternity.

It was he who finally looked away. The older man was speaking to him, unaware that anything earth-shattering had just occurred. Alex saw Michael make the first move, further into the room, his companion advancing with him. Their progress was slowed by people stopping them to talk, but Alex knew what their destination was. Although Michael did not look her way again, she had no doubt that, in a few moments, she would be face to face with him.

And then? What would he say to her? How would he greet her, in front of other people? Her imagination ran riot. . . 'Hello, darling, how have you been?' Or perhaps, with that zany sense of humour of his, 'Hello, darling, *where* have you been?'

How had he managed to find out where she was? She thought she had covered her tracks so well. And what was she doing here?

Doug Weston supplied the answer to her last question. 'That must be our new locum with Charles,' he said. 'He was due to fly in this afternoon.'

A locum? How on earth had he managed to arrange a locum in Mackay at such short notice? After all, it was only two weeks since she herself had known she was coming here.

One thing—locums could be quite short, as short as a week, even. But that hope was dashed as Doug Weston continued, 'Charles—that's Charles Evans, our senior partner—is going to the States for a couple of months soon. If appearances are anything to go by, he's done a good job of finding a fill-in.' His hand went up, automatically, to straighten his black tie as the other doctors approached. Again, just a few feet away, they were halted by an effusive elderly lady who held them talking for several minutes. Alex realised she had missed her chance to turn and lose herself in the crowd. Anyway, that would only have postponed the inevitable. Michael had determination written in every line of his face. And once he had his mind made up about anything. . .!

So? She too had a mind of her own. She was glad she had stood her ground. Glad, also, that she was wearing a dress Michael had not seen before. It was a deep fuchsia-pink silk which she had bought in Rome and she knew it did all the right things for her. If only she had not, at the last minute, decided to wear the diamond pendant. He *would* recognise that—and remember the night he had given it to her.

She remembered it too. Her cheeks flamed suddenly and she had to push aside thoughts that would only make her vulnerable. She lifted her head and there was a challenge in her eyes as Alex watched him take the last few steps that brought him to stand in front of her.

Anyone watching would have seen only a handsome-man-meets-pretty-girl scenario. Alex wondered whether Michael's thoughts behind his calm façade were as chaotic as hers.

Dr Evans also had an appreciative gleam in his eye as he looked at Alex. But he turned and introduced his junior partner to the new locum. The two younger men shook hands, then Doug Weston said, 'This is Alex. . .' he hesitated, clearly unable to recall her surname, then continued '. . .one of the sisters at the hospital.'

Dr Evans extended his hand to her, but Alex pretended not to see it. If she shook his hand, she would have to shake Michael's as well, and she shrank from that contact. She nodded and smiled briefly, without actually looking at Michael, then realised she was holding her breath as she waited for his response.

He said, 'Haven't we met somewhere? Your face seems so familiar. . .'

Alex breathed a little more freely. He might be going to play games with her—that would be in character—but he hadn't betrayed their relationship—not yet, at least!

She looked him in the eye and murmured, 'One forgets so easily.'

His mouth twitched briefly. 'Doesn't one!' he agreed, then added, 'I didn't catch your Christian name.'

That was almost her undoing. She should have remembered he was so much better at gamesmanship than she. His last words, as he knew very well, were the identical ones he had used the first time they had met, over two years ago. It had been at a hospital dance and he had turned her world upside-down, then. And here he was turning it upside-down again.

He was waiting for her to tell him her name. Coherent thought forsook her. All she could think of were the words with which she had answered him on that first occasion, an eternity ago, it seemed.

'My name is Alex,' she said, and knew what he would say next. It was as though they were repeating lines, learned long ago and familiar, for some stage show.

'Alex?' he asked. 'Is that for Alexandra, as in Princess? Or for Alexis, as in *Dynasty*?'

There was a glint of sardonic amusement in his eye as he waited for her reply.

'My name is Alexandra—Alexandra McLachlan.'

Again, that was word for word what she had said then. But this time it seemed to cause him some surprise, as if he had expected something different. His eyebrow shot upwards and he seemed momentarily at a loss for words. Grasping her opportunity, Alex said, 'If you'll excuse

me,' then turned and plunged into the crowd. Fran
Powers, with whom she had been working in the past
week, grabbed her by the arm, drew her into her group
and introduced her around. She hoped Michael was
watching, so that he could see her laughing and talking
as though she hadn't a care in the world.

She managed to keep up the charade through dinner,
talking with Dr Evans on her left hand and a male nurse
whose name she could not remember on her right. Once
or twice she lost the thread of the conversation and
hoped nobody noticed. She did not know where Michael
was sitting or with whom. She *did* know that, before the
party was over, he would make or find an opportunity to
talk to her.

He waited until the meal was almost finished. Some of
the guests were still drinking coffee at their tables.
Others were on the dance floor. Alex heard his voice
behind her and had to control a sudden shakiness of the
hand that held her coffee cup.

'Would you care to dance?'

Carefully she replaced the cup on its saucer. Dr Evans,
beside her, was smiling up at Michael and then at Alex,
waiting for her response. To refuse to dance would
attract attention, and she did not want that. She gave a
tiny nod, stood up and walked on to the floor. There she
had no choice but to turn and face Michael.

He moved forward and his arm encircled her waist
and his hand clasped the one she raised to his. She was
stiff and unyielding and her steps were faltering at first.
But then, without warning, her resistance melted away
before a quite irrational surge of contentment. If she had
analysed her feelings, she would have confessed that she
felt as though she had come home after being away for a
very long time. She relaxed against him with a tiny sigh,

felt his arm tighten about her and the familiar hardness of his body close against hers. Their steps now were in perfect unison, as they always had been when they danced together.

Her mental aberration lasted a few minutes. Then she tried to pull away, but Michael's arm was firm and strong. As she persisted, he did at last loosen his hold, drawing back without losing the rhythm of the dance and looking down at her with mocking eyes. They danced for a little while longer, stiffly and apart. Then, almost inaudibly, she said, 'I have to talk to you.'

That too was unpremeditated. To talk to him was really the last thing she wanted to do.

He murmured, close to her ear, 'Better late than never, I guess,' pivoted deftly and guided her between tables and through an open door leading on to a balcony. There, finally, he released her.

Alex moved a little way along the balcony, to where they could not be seen through overlooking windows, and stood clasping the rail of the balcony and looking out beyond the cars parked along the street below to the darkness that was the ocean. A warm breeze, soft as a zephyr, caressed her cheeks and lifted her hair slightly from her bare shoulders.

He came and stood beside her and with one finger turned her face to him, studying it for a moment as if to see what changes time had wrought there. Then he ran his finger caressingly across her forehead and down her cheek, following the line of her hair. In the soft half-light that came through the drawn curtains, Alex could see his features dimly. There was no tenderness in them. And none in his voice as he said, 'You're as lovely as ever.' It was as though he had made a clinical assessment after examining a patient.

She jerked her head away and said angrily, 'Don't do that!'

'Sorry, Princess! You used to like it.'

'And don't call me that!'

He shrugged. 'You wanted to talk?'

She drew a deep breath and said, almost inaudibly, 'How dare you?'

'How dare *I*?' His voice too was low, almost gentle, but the emphasis on the last word was unmistakable. Alex turned her head away, biting her lip.

'How dare I what?' he insisted.

'Follow me here.'

'Is that what you think I did?'

'What else am I to think?'

Michael shrugged again. 'Still the same old pathological tendency to jump to conclusions!'

She ignored the jibe. 'Do you expect me to believe your turning up here is pure coincidence?'

'Believe what you like! A more rational assumption might be that we both read the same medical journal. And that we both had reasons for wanting to get away from Sydney for a while—whatever those reasons were. . .?'

She ignored the query in his voice. She had no intention of being sidetracked into a discussion of her reasons for leaving Sydney. She wanted to know what he intended to do, now that they were both here.

'All right,' she admitted reluctantly. 'I'll accept that you didn't know I was here. But you can't possibly stay. . .not now.'

'Oh! Why not?'

'It would be intolerable.'

'For whom?'

She almost said, 'for both of us', but stopped herself.

Perhaps he would not find it intolerable. Perhaps he no longer cared enough for her presence to matter.

When she did not answer, he said, 'I certainly have no intention of fabricating a sudden recall to Sydney.'

'Nor do I,' Alex assured him.

'Then we have two alternatives. Either we stay and tell people the truth—and there's nothing so terrible in that—people split up all the time. Or we stay and don't tell anyone anything.'

His first alternative was quite unthinkable. She could not stay and work here, among all these people who were still strangers, and have them knowing. . .talking.

'You mean. . .pretend. . .to be strangers?'

'Something like that.'

'Do you mind?'

'If you mean, do I mind acting a part. . .' He shrugged as though it was no big deal. 'If you mean, do I mind what's happened. . . I'm not sure. That's what I came up here to sort out. I'm beginning to think it might just have been the best thing that could have happened.'

Alex gave a small anguished sound which she quickly stifled. He seemed not to have heard but said lightly, 'Now, I suggest we return to the party, before people begin to read a budding romance into this tête-à-tête in the moonlight.'

He looked down at her with a lopsided grin, then his face hardened and his hand went out and grasped her arm tightly.

'But first,' he said, 'I think we have some unfinished business.'

Before she could protest, his arms were round her, vicelike, drawing him to her so that once again she could feel the hard, lean, uncompromising strength of him. She fought against him, but, when his mouth came down on hers, her resistance evaporated. Her mind told her that this should not be happening, but her body was playing her false and she could not help herself. She allowed herself to melt against him, as she had done in the dance, while her mouth responded to his kisses. Her arms went up and encircled his neck.

With her yielding came self-doubt that was akin to panic. Had she, after all, made a terrible mistake when she had walked out of his life? When she was away from him it all seemed so clear-cut. But when he was here, like this, kissing her, logic and reason evaporated. Oh, why had he come!

Michael held her just long enough for them both to be perfectly aware of her response. Then he released her slowly, holding her away from him, but his lips continued to tease hers, lightly, tantalisingly. The mockery in his eyes when he at last released her told her that he knew perfectly well that her body was clamouring to be close to his still.

Alex realised then what he had been doing. He was making the point, as clearly as he knew how, that this time *he* was rejecting *her*.

When finally he let go of her arms, she almost overbalanced, but he appeared not to notice and walked away from her.

She wanted to cry. She wanted to hit him. She stood where he had left her until she heard him say, 'Coming?'

As she moved unsteadily towards him, he turned and looked down at her. His face softened and there was almost a hint of apology in his voice as he asked, 'Are you all right?'

She nodded mutely, raised her head, turned and walked back into the reception-room. The music was playing and the floor was crowded with dancers as she made her way to her table. Michael followed her, drew out her chair and, when she was seated said, 'Thank you,' politely, and walked away.

Fortunately, the chairs on either side of her were vacant. A waitress appeared and offered her coffee. By the time the music stopped and Fran Powers slipped into a chair beside her, Alex felt almost composed. Which was as well, because Fran was clearly agog to hear all about the new doctor.

Fran was a nice person, friendly and outgoing, and Alex had enjoyed working with her. But she had shown a lively curiosity about Alex's personal life, which Alex's evasive answers had only served to increase. Alex knew she was in for an inquisition now. To delay it, she said, 'You're looking very nice tonight.' Fran was too, in a vivid emerald-green dress which brought out the highlights in her bouncy auburn curls and deep brown eyes.

'Thank you,' Fran responded, but was not about to be sidetracked. 'Now, tell me all about the new locum. What did you find out about him?'

'Not much, really. I asked him how he came to be here.' That at least was the truth!

'Oh? And how did he?'

'Like most of us, he reads the positions vacant ads in medical journals,' Alex said.

'And where is he from?'

'Sydney.'

'Is he married?'

'He didn't say.'

Fran sighed. 'I guess we'll find out sooner or later.'

I sincerely hope not, thought Alex.

'You and he looked so right, dancing together,' Fran went on dreamily. 'I do hope he's not married.'

'He *is* a good dancer,' admitted Alex.

'So are you. And when he danced you out on to the balcony, every female in the room was green with envy!'

If only they'd known! thought Alex.

'Was it romantic. . .out there in the moonlight? What did you talk about?' asked Fran egaerly.

'Oh, this and that.'

Alex had to terminate this awkward conversation somehow. At the risk of offending Fran, she said, rather sharply, 'If you want the truth, I thought he was pushy and much too self-assured. And the less I see of him around the hospital, the better I'll be pleased.'

Fran could have no possible idea how true that was! She gave Alex a long, hard look but, before she could say anything more, Doug Weston appeared and asked Alex to dance. Alex accepted with an alacrity that clearly delighted that young man. He had no idea that what made him an acceptable partner at the moment was that he was an uninspired conversationalist who was unlikely to ask awkward questions.

The evening dragged on.

Alex caught glimpses of Michael, sitting at a table with several other men. He seemed not to be taking much part in their conversation, which was unusual for him. He didn't dance again, and that too was not like him.

Later she saw a waitress approach and speak to Dr Evans, who nodded, stood up and walked quickly out of the room. He reappeared after a few minutes and spoke briefly to the men at the table. Michael said something in reply, Dr Evans seemed to remonstrate, then give in. Michael stood up and the two of them departed. Alex deduced that Dr Evans had been called to a patient and that Michael had insisted on going along too.

Before long, Alex sought out Fran and told her she was tired, was going back to the home and would see her tomorrow. As she found her car and drove the short distance to the hospital, she felt more than just tired; she felt totally exhausted.

In her room, as she undressed and hung her lovely dress in the wardrobe, she realised how much had changed in the hours since she had put it on. She had been so confident then. Now all her hopes, all her plans for the future had collapsed about her feet, like a house of cards. Her future, now, was as uncertain as it ever had been.

But, as she leaned across and switched off her bedside light, she chuckled suddenly. Michael's outrageous plan to behave like strangers when they met would certainly add a touch of spice to life in Mackay!

If he ran true to form, that was something she could safely bet on.

CHAPTER TWO

THE formal opening of the Mackay Community Hospital took place at three o'clock the following afternoon, in the large foyer of the hospital, and was attended by a throng of official guests and VIPs.

Alex didn't need Fran's nudge to tell her when Michael arrived.

'He looks just as distinguished as he did last night in his dinner suit,' Fran murmured admiringly.

Today Michael was wearing a dark grey lounge suit. Alex could have told Fran, to the day, how old the suit was, along with its size, and the brand name of the shirt he wore with it.

She avoided looking in his drection but was aware that he was being hailed by a group of men, probably doctors, and was not surprised to hear, a moment to two later, a shout of laughter coming from that direction.

Fran was still gazing at Michael. 'All that gorgeous masculinity and a sense of humour too!' she sighed soulfully. 'You don't think you could have been mistaken about him last night?'

Alex was spared having to answer that by a crackle from the PA system and the start of the official formalities. She tried to concentrate, but she was tense and restless and the speeches were boring. The only difference between them, she decided, was that some were congratulatory and the others self-congratulatory— depending on who was the speaker. She was glad when they were over and she could move around, with other nurses, serving afternoon tea and chatting to the guests.

But all the time she was aware of Michael, while being careful that their paths did not cross. Fran had no such inhibitions. Alex saw her talking and laughing with him for much longer than it took for him to make a selection from her plate of hors d'oeuvre. There were still stars in Fran's eyes when Alex met up with her some minutes later.

'I'm *sure* you were wrong about Michael Jones,' Fran assured Alex earnestly. 'He's so nice, and not at all self-opinionated as you said.' She floated away, on a cloud nine all of her own.

Alex realised that she not only had her own situation to worry about, but also Fran's. It wouldn't be fair to let Fran fall prey to Michael's charms, as she seemed in imminent danger of doing. Alex knew how quickly that could happen and how difficult it was to disentangle oneself once it had happened. She was going to have to do a more convincing job than she had hitherto, in convincing Fran that it was wise to avoid falling in love with Dr Michael Jones.

Reluctantly she decided the only thing to do was to tell Fran at least a part of the truth about Michael.

When afternoon tea was finished, the guests were taken, in small groups led by staff members, on tours of the hospital.

Alex found herself allotted two elderly couples and a middle-aged lady. They were all very quiet, seemingly overawed by the occasion, and Alex felt that her task as a tour guide should not be too demanding.

She introduced herself to them and was shepherding them towards the door when Michael appeared.

'Mind if I tag along, Sister?' he asked meekly.

Alex suspected that the meekness was deceptive, but there was a flutter from the ladies at the thought of a nice-looking young man going along, and she could think of no plausible reason to refuse him. She nodded briefly but did not introduce him to the others.

Self-opening doors separated the foyer from the hospital wards. She led the way into a share room and then a private suite. There were 'oohs' and 'aahs' of appreciation of the beautiful décor and appointments, and Alex had only to smile and agree. Michael said nothing for a while and the elderly ladies tried to draw him into their conversation. Clearly they had no idea he was a doctor. As the tour proceeded, he added an inane 'ooh' and 'aah' or two of his own. Alex shot him a disapproving glare which he returned with a stare of blank innocence.

Gradually the ladies relaxed and became more talkative. Most of their remarks were prefaced by phrases such as, 'When I had my big operation. . .' or 'My doctor says. . .' They were enjoying themselves, and Alex let them chatter on and kept her tour-guide patter to a minimum. But when Michael, replying to a remark by one of the ladies, said, 'Really? How very interesting! Now, when *I* had *my*. . .' Alex turned on him such a quelling glance that he subsided into an incoherent mumble and even she had to feign a fit of coughing to camouflage an almost irrepressible desire to laugh.

The other two men had been quiet so far. Obviously they were well used to leaving the floor to their wives. But when Alex took them into a treatment-room one of them, Mr Southwold, admitted to being a retired engineer and asked some intelligent questions which Alex answered to the best of her ability.

She was in the middle of her explanation when she happened to glance at Michael, and immediately wished she had not done so. He was standing behind the others, leaning lazily against a doorframe. His mouth had the lopsided, upward tilt that she knew from experience presaged mischief. His eyes, wickedly aglint, were looking her up and down in such a manner that she felt, suddenly, as if she were wearing transparent gauze, instead of a demure white, quite opaque uniform.

She lost her train of thought, hesitated, stammered, and, to give herself time to recover, had to ask Mr Southwold to repeat his question.

She was careful not to look in Michael's direction again and, as soon as possible, moved her group along. She wished fervently that the inspection were over, because she felt sure Michael had more mischief in mind.

She was right. Having embarrassed her once, he went on to follow up his advantage. In the meekest of voices and looking very innocent and serious, he began asking questions, as though he knew nothing at all about hospitals or the medical profession. His questions were harmless enough at first, but gradually became more and more outrageous. Alex retaliated as best she could by answering him in words of one syllable, as though she were explaining things to a not-very-bright schoolboy. She was delighted to see that that was how the other members of the group were beginning to regard him. She could almost read their thoughts in their interchanged glances. Such a handsome young man too! What a pity. . .!

But when, in an ante-room in OR, he pointed to a Foley's catheter and asked, 'And what is that used for, Sister?' she turned her back, without answering, and said to the others, 'Now, shall we all go into the operating-room?' They reacted with interest and surged forward. Behind their backs, Alex cast a look at Michael which would have slain a lesser mortal. He grinned back at her innocently.

Alex informed her group that here was where she worked herself, and they were suitably impressed. Michael said solemnly, 'What a lot of responsibility you must have, Sister. And you so young! Don't you ever feel like running away from it all?'

Alex seethed inwardly but replied, evenly enough, 'My *hospital work* has never got me down to that extent.'

He said, 'Oh? I'm glad! You obviously give your work a high priority in your life. Haven't you ever felt like getting married?'

The two older women made indignant, clucking sounds, indicating that they considered his questions were becoming much too personal. Alex replied in a chillingly formal voice and an accent acquired at Sydney's most exclusive private school, 'If I ever did contemplate such a thing, I've thought better of it since. My career is my life from now on.'

That sounded horribly pious, but it was greeted by an instant murmur of approval from all her hearers, except one. As the others nodded their heads and smiled approvingly at one another, Michael, visibly subdued, shrugged and murmured, 'Pity!'

From then on he was silent. Finally the tour was over and they were standing in a little group in the foyer again. Everyone said, 'Thank you, Sister,' cordially and Michael added, 'Yes, thank you, Sister. It's been most entertaining.'

Alex looked him straight in the eye and said, in a clear, penetrating voice that the others could not fail to hear, 'I'm glad you enjoyed it, *Doctor*. And I'm happy to have been able to fill in some of the gaps in your medical knowledge.'

She turned on her heel and walked away, but not before she heard the exclamations of surprise from the other members of the group, and the beginning of Michael's abashed attempt to explain to them who he was. Alex resisted the temptation to look back over her shoulder and observe his discomfiture. But she could not resist thinking gleefully to herself, Well, Dr Jones, there are five patients who are unlikely to bring their medical problems to *you*!

There was no sign of Fran in the foyer. Some of the guests had left already; others lingered talking. Although it was not part of her duties, Alex busied herself gathering glasses on to trays, until Fran appeared, with her group of tourists. As soon as Fran was free, Alex went to her and said, 'I'm going across to shower and change, Fran. There's something I'd like to talk to you about,' then, realising that Fran was looking almost as exhausted as she herself felt, she added, 'Unless, of course, you feel like crashing, stat?'

'I think I could just about manage to lie on a couch and listen. I certainly can't promise scintillating conversation—I've scintillated enough for one day. What an effort!'

'I know how you feel. But don't worry, I promise I'll do most of the talking.'

'I'm surprised you're still capable. OK. I'll see you soon, then,' Fran said.

Alex left immediately, and was careful not to look about her until she was safely away. She didn't know whether Michael was still around, and she didn't want to know. She showered and pulled on jeans and a large, loose cotton shirt.

When Fran appeared she was also in jeans, with a pale green polo-shirt, and she was carrying a small tray holding two full glasses with ice clinking in them. Also on the tray was a plateful of dainty sandwiches and appetising titbits, obviously left-overs from afternoon tea.

Alex raised enquiring eyebrows at the drinks and Fran said, 'G and Ts. I think we've earned them!'

'Great!'

Alex took a glass, placed it carefully on a small bedside table, then piled pillows on the bed and flopped down against them. Fran sat down in the big cane easy chair with its comfortable cushions, tucked her legs under her and sighed. 'How did your tour go?' she asked. 'I saw Michael Jones going off with your group. I think you've got yourself an admirer.' She sounded envious.

Alex leaned forward and took a sandwich from the tray. 'I'll tell you about my tour later on. You'll appreciate its finer points after you've heard something else I've got to say. Anyway, I saw *you* talking to him for quite a while. Did you find out anything more about him?'

'Not really. He was very charming and easy to talk to. But he backed off as soon as I asked him anything about himself. Quite mysterious, actually. . .'

Alex could see that the element of mystery about Michael only added to his charm in Fran's eyes. She was glad she had decided to talk to her.

'Don't go falling for Michael Jones, Fran,' she warned.

Fran looked surprised. 'I haven't thought that far ahead yet. But why shouldn't I, just supposing. . .?'

'Because he isn't. . .available.'

'How do you know?'

'Actually, I know quite a lot about him,' said Alex. 'You see, I'm married to him.'

She almost laughed out loud to see the variety of

expressions that flashed across Fran's face—amazement, curiosity, disappointment, envy. . .

'Well!' Fran said at length, on a long, expiring breath. 'You're absolutely sure about this? It couldn't be a case of mistaken identity, I suppose?' she asked, clinging to one last slender straw.

Alex shook her head slowly.

'I didn't think so,' said Fran ruefully. 'Well, don't just sit there! Tell me. . .the whole story.'

'That's what I asked you to come round for. I felt bad not telling you last night, but I was in a complete state of shock, practically catatonic, in fact, seeing him here, and I needed time to collect my wits.'

'You mean you had no idea he was coming here?'

Alex shook her head.

'How long since you've seen him?' asked Fran.

'Three months, one week and five days.'

'You're still counting? That probably means you're still hurting.'

'I thought I was starting not to, but now. . .' Alex raised her shoulders in a despairing little shrug.

'Is there any chance of a reconciliation? Perhaps now you're both here. . .?'

'I doubt it.'

'But why? He's so. . .so everything! And *you* wouldn't come last in a beauty contest either,' Fran added.

Alex shrugged again. 'It's the old story—another woman. An old girlfriend of his, actually. I wonder, now, whether they ever really stopped seeing one another.' She was silent, remembering. Then she went on. 'I was so rapt, swept off my feet. We had a whirlwind romance and were married before I had time to think. It was all so exciting. I was so sure he loved me. I can see now that I was just plain stupid—naïve. Anyway, I've learned my lesson. Never again.'

'Oh, come on! Never's a long time, you know.'

'Oh, I don't mean I'll never fall in love again. But never again with my eyes shut. Next time I'll be very wide awake, very cautious.'

'How long did it last?' asked Fran.

'Almost two years. But the rot began to set in some time before the end.'

The rot—that was what it was—the rot of rumour, suspicion and jealousy.

First came the rumours. There had been people in the hospital who had been only too ready to hint to Alex— for her own good, of course—that Michael was seeing Leonie Tyson again. At first, she'd been too much in love, too deliriously happy, to believe what they were saying. After all, anyone who was not married to Michael was bound to be jealous.

But the rumours persisted and the doubts grew. Inevitably, their relationship suffered. From snatching every moment together that their times off duty allowed, Michael began to make excuses—pressure of work—a patient needing him—he couldn't study at home because she was too distracting and when they were together he only wanted to make love to her. Later, the excuse was that the noise of her clattering in the kitchen disturbed him. He took to staying overnight in the residents' quarters more often.

Knowing the pressures on a Registrar of Surgery in a big, busy hospital, Alex made allowances.

But then, one night towards the end, she arrived home, thoroughly exhausted after a late shift. She had expected that Michael would have been there, perhaps with a drink and even a snack ready for her.

Instead she found the apartment a mess. It had been broken into and ransacked. She had been so upset she had done what she knew he didn't like her to do—she had tried to reach him at the hospital. But he was not on the ward, not in the quarters, not due in, they told her, until the morning.

Trying not to face the truth still, Alex tried to assess the damage. Their TV and almost new video cassette recorder had been taken, also Michael's compact disc player, which was his pride and joy. Alex spent a sleepless night, and went on duty next morning feeling completely drained. She had finished a midwifery course not long before and was now staffing in obstets. They had a hectic day, some difficult deliveries, post-natal complications, demanding mothers, crying babies. She didn't even manage a lunch break, and it was not until she went off duty in mid-afternoon that she was able to go in search of Michael.

He could only spare her a few snatched moments in a utility-room. She charged him, first, with his where-abouts last night, and his answers completely failed to put her doubts to rest. He had forgotten he had said he would be home. He had been held up at work with an emergency, after which he had gone to the residents' sitting-room and fallen asleep on a couch.

When she told him about the break-in he was upset that she had not notified the police immediately—what was she thinking about—didn't she know that was the very first thing one did?

At that point, his beeper sounded. He seemed relieved and told her he would see her at home as soon as he could get there. In the meantime, would she ring the police, please—at once!

When he did come home, he was penitent and attentive. He had brought her flowers. They talked—really talked—for the first time in weeks and made love before falling asleep in each other's arms.

It was wonderful, and Alex forgave him fully and tried to forget. For a time things really did improve. . .

Alex came to a halt in her narration, seeming barely to remember that Fran was there, sitting quietly in her chair, her eyes sympathetic, concerned for her friend. After several minutes, Fran prompted gently, 'So what happened—after that—to cause the final break?'

'I found a note. . .from Leonie Tyson, his old girlfriend, which said it all. I suppose it just confirmed everything I'd suspected. I didn't wait to confront him with it. I rang the hospital to say I was sick, and just packed my things and left. A few days later, I sent a letter of resignation to the hospital. And that was that—until last night.'

'You mean you haven't spoken to him, or made contact at all, since you left?'

'No. I just couldn't face the possibility of another row.'

'And didn't he try to find you?'

'Oh, yes,' said Alex. 'But I made it hard for him. I knew he would expect me to go to Avonleigh, my grandmother's place on the Darling Downs. So I stayed away from there. I told them I'd left him, but not much about why, and I asked them not to tell him where I was. Not that he was likely to have followed me, anyway, even if they had told him.'

'Why? Where were you?' Fran was curious.

'With a friend who was studying art in Perugia, in Italy. To pass the time, I did a short course in Italian at the Università di Stranieri. By the time I came back to Australia it was safe to go to Avonleigh.'

'*Had* he tried to find you there?'

'Yes. My mother said he'd been there and had rung numerous times, at first, then seemed to give up. I stayed there until I got fed up with doing nothing but sit around and listen to my mother and Gran commiserate, so I went back to Sydney with the intention of getting back into nursing. And here I am.'

'And here he is!'

'Exactly! Here he is! So what do I do now? On second thoughts,' Alex laughed, 'don't answer that! I didn't ask you here for advice, or to weep on your shoulder. I know I'll have to work it out for myself. I just wanted you to know why you shouldn't get involved with Michael—at least, not yet.'

'I'm afraid I wouldn't know what advice to give you, even if you did ask me. Except, perhaps, that you should get together and talk,' said Fran.

'What's the use? We'd only fight.'

'But the poor guy doesn't seem to have had a chance to defend himself, or explain anything. People *can* jump to some pretty far-off conclusions, you know.'

'I know, but not in this case. That note was nothing if not conclusive.'

'Does he know you saw the note?'

'Probably not.'

'Where did you find it?' asked Fran.

'In the pocket of his jacket.'

Fran raised her eyebrows and Alex was quick to read her mind.

'No, I wasn't snooping. I was emptying out the pockets before taking the jacket to the cleaners.'

'Then I think at least he should know that you saw the note, and have a chance to explain it.'

'I realise we'll have to talk sooner or later,' Alex admitted. 'But right now, I don't feel I can face it. Anyway, thanks for listening. And be careful, huh?'

'Of course.'

'You won't tell anyone else?'

'Of course not. But how are you going to get around not telling people you know one another? Won't *he* do that?'

'He agreed not to. In fact, it was his idea that we just pretend not to know one another—strangers when we meet, sort of thing.'

'Do you really think you can carry that off?' asked Fran.

'For a while, anyway—though, after this afternoon, I'm beginning to see it might not be all that easy.'

'You mean the guided tour? What happened?'

Alex, feeling as though a load had been lifted just as a result of having talked to Fran, gave such a comical account of Michael's antics and her revenge that they were both soon laughing helplessly.

'I knew he had a sense of humour,' gasped Fran, when she could speak. 'I just can't decide who came off best in the end. A Foley's catheter! What a hoot! It would have served him right if you'd explained to him, then and there, in great detail.'

That started them off again. Eventually Fran said, 'You realise, of course, that he'll probably be in OR tomorrow morning? Charles Evans is doing a hernia repair and he's bound to bring Michael along to observe.'

'As long as they don't decide to use a Foley's. . . Oh, I mustn't laugh any more—my side's aching already. I

really thought this was going to be a serious session!'
laughed Alex.

'I must say I've never enjoyed anyone weeping on my
shoulder so much,' said Fran. 'You *will* keep me
informed of future developments, won't you? I wouldn't
miss them for the world!'

Fran departed, with a final, delighted chuckle. Alex
remained where she was, squatting on the bed, her knees
up to her chin and her arms clasped around them.

Talking and laughing with Fran had dispersed some
of the despondency that had descended on her from time
to time since last evening. And it was reassuring to know
that Fran did not consider Alex's problems insoluble.
Clearly she thought some good old-fashioned communi-
cation was indicated.

Alex knew that Fran was right, as far as she was able
to judge. But Fran only knew part of the story. There
was more, much more, that Alex had not told her. This
was not just a simple eternal triangle that could be
resolved, step by step, with a neat little QED inserted at
the end. This was more complicated.

The half of the story which Alex had not told Fran
related to money. And Alex even now was not at all sure
that she had handled that part of her relationship with
Michael wisely. She had asked herself over and over, in
the last few months, what difference it would have made
had she told Michael everything from the beginning.

The reason she had, time and again, put off doing it
was Michael's attitude to money. He came from what he
was proud to call 'humble beginnings', and had a plank-
sized chip on his shoulder about doctors whose way up
the professional ladder was nicely oiled by 'filthy lucre'.
Everyone in the hospital knew that. What nobody knew

was that Alex had lots of filthy lucre—pots of it, in fact, in bank accounts, investments and property holdings.

She had grown up with the trappings of wealth all around her, had lived in an exclusive Sydney suburb, went to the best private school, spent holidays in Europe and weekends on the family yacht.

Her father had died when she was sixteen and when she turned eighteen she decided to do something worthwhile with her life, not just live on the fruits of her father's success. She applied to enter nursing training and, motivated partly by youthful idealism and partly by a hard-nosed realisation that money did not always lead to genuine relationships with one's peers, she resolved to say nothing about her circumstances but to live, as most of the other nurses did, on their nurse's pay.

After a few initial shocks, which made her realise what an ivory-tower existence she had lived until now, she took to nursing like a duck to water and, apart from the occasional consultation which her financial adviser demanded, she managed, quite successfully, to forget that she did not really have to make do on her pay packet.

She had just finished her three years' training and begun twelve months of staffing when she met Michael and fell in love with him, as he with her, at first sight. It crossed her mind a few times that she was not being completely open in not telling him about her money. But it had all happened so quickly that she still felt almost a stranger to him in some respects. Also, knowing his oft-expressed views about money, she was afraid that if she told him the truth it would spoil things for them.

Before she knew it they were married and it became even harder to say anything. And, too, she was still working at the hospital, with friends who had, all along, accepted her at face value. She couldn't face telling them that she had been living a lie for three years. She kept putting off talking to Michael, as she knew she should. Anyway, there were too few occasions for them to talk. They were living in a small apartment near the hospital, or rather, Alex was living there and Michael was there as often as his duties as a resident at the hospital allowed.

When their relationship began to deteriorate, Alex knew she could not add extra pressure to the marriage by telling him she had married him under false pretences.

Then, once the doubt about him and Leonie Tyson began to eat at her mind like a cancer, it was easy to wonder whether he had known all along about her money. Why else, if he was still in love with Leonie, would he have married Alex? He made no secret of the fact that he wanted to buy into a private practice. How better to facilitate that than to marry a rich wife? And better still if he could say that he had not known she was rich when he married her. That way, no one could accuse him of having double standards.

So things had gone from bad to worse.

Until, finally, the note.

Leonie Tyson had a dinstinctive, frilly handwriting which one always recognised in reports and case-notes. Alex did not have to look at the signature to know whose it was when she found the note. Leonie had written:

Dear Mike,
Please don't feel guilty about last night—it wasn't your fault. Wish I could help more. Pity I'm not as rich as you-know-who. Time will help there.

Luv, Le.

Alex felt her suspicions were confirmed on both counts—beyond doubt, beyond hope. Michael *was* seeing Leonie. And he *did* know about her money.

She couldn't face accusations and explanations. She didn't want to see in his face the confirmation of her fears. She packed her bags and left.

It was the end of their 'perfect' marriage.

Alex stirred and sighed. It was not literally the end of their marriage. She was still, legally, Alexandra Jones. She had known all along she would ultimately have to do something about that. Eventually, at a nice safe distance, she would have started divorce proceedings. But now. . .?

She felt incredibly weary all at once—unable to ask momentous questions, let alone solve them. She'd have to let things slide for the time being, just go along with Michael's plan and hope that eventually. . .

She had no idea what she hoped.

CHAPTER THREE

THERE were several reasons why the nurses in OR had pre-operative jitters on Monday morning.

For a start, it was a historic occasion. At eight o'clock the first operation in the new hospital would begin. It was only a humble repair of an inguinal hernia, but it would be the first time the girls had worked together as a team and so it would be a demonstration of each one's capabilities. Then, too, they would be working with surgeons whose methods, likes and dislikes were quite unknown to them, and that was always a challenge. For Alex, it would be a test of how effective the preparation of the theatre she and Fran had been engaged in during the past week would prove.

On top of this, Alex had reasons unknown to anybody else for feeling apprehensive. Dr Evans would almost certainly be accompanied by his new locum this morning. Which meant that Alex would be working side by side with a husband who she had to pretend was a stranger, and who could well be seeking revenge for the humiliating set-down she had administered to him yesterday afternoon. He had deserved it, of course, but she doubted whether he would remember that if an opportunity presented itself to get even with her.

Then, too, strangely enough, this would be the first time she and Michael had actually worked together. Alex had finished her OR training before Michael began his residency and, when she had first met him, she had begun her course in obstetrics and had continued there throughout the two years of their ill-fated marriage.

So Alex was having a quite unusual attack of nerves. Well before eight o'clock she had personally checked and rechecked everything in the unit—lights, oxygen, suction apparatus, temperature, humidity, sterile packs. . . She made a minute adjustment to the light above the operating table. But when she switched on the light of the X-ray viewing screen, which would not by any stretch of the imagination be used for a herniorrhaphy, and caught her nurses exchanging understanding smiles, she laughed and said, 'I think we could all use a cup of coffee. We've just got time.'

The coffee helped a little and filled in the time before Alex had to don cap and mask and go into the scrubroom.

She had lathered her hands and arms and was reaching for a brush when she heard the squeak of rubber-soled shoes on the polished floor outside and the murmur of deep voices before the door of the surgeons' changeroom closed. Almost immediately there was the noise of tyres in the theatre next door and of nurses' voices reassuring the patient as he was transferred from trolley to table.

The arrival of the patient worked wonders for Alex, reminding her that she was a trained and competent member of a surgical team with a job to do. The wellbeing of the patient was all that mattered.

Soon the doors of the scrub-room swung open and two tall figures in loose green cotton trousers and shortsleeved tops entered. Caps hid their hair and masks covered most of their faces, but Alex caught the flash of surprise in Michael's eyes as he caught sight of her. Dr Evans had, as expected, brought his locum along this morning, and his locum had obviously not expected to see his wife standing at the bowl in the corner, rhythmically scrubbing away.

Dr Evans said cheerfully, 'Good morning, Sister. I think you've met Michael Jones. . .yes, of course, at the staff party. Good show, that!'

Alex murmured, 'Yes, it was. Good morning, Dr Jones.'

Michael responded quite naturally, 'Hello there again, Sister!' as he and Dr Evans ranged themselves at bowls. Above the sound of running water, they resumed a conversation they had apparently been having, discussing the medical problems of a family that Dr Evans would be handing over to Michael after his departure for overseas.

As Alex turned and reached for a sterile towel to dry her arms and hands, Michael flicked a glance at her, but Alex could read nothing in it. She was gowned and gloved and standing waiting, with her hands raised to shoulder height, when the men turned from their basins to the tables where the sterile packs awaited. The scout nurse tied Charles Evans's gown, then he slipped into his gloves with accustomed ease and walked through into the theatre. Alex heard him talking to the anaesthetist about the patient, who was now unconscious.

The scout tied Michael's gown but, instead of putting on his own gloves as Charles had done, he gestured for Alex to hold them for him. Some surgeons did require this of their sterile nurse. Alex had no way of knowing whether it was Michael's usual practice, but she had no choice but to co-operate. She indicated by a flick of her head that the scout nurse could go through into theatre, then wished she had not done so. As soon as they were alone, Michael moved a few inches nearer to her.

'I need to talk to you,' he said in a low voice.

The atmosphere between them was as taut as the glove Alex was holding, waiting for him to slip his hand into. Her voice was taut too, and pitched a little higher than usual as she replied, 'Certainly, Doctor, as long as it relates to the patient.'

He sighed. 'No, Duchess, I can't rightly say it does.'

His shoulders slumped and he turned and walked away from her.

Alex followed him through into the theatre and, for a moment or two, found it impossible to keep her mind on the patient, as she had admonished him to do. 'Duchess!' He had always called her that, instead of his usual 'Princess', when she was standing on her dignity. Memory threatened to overwhelm her.

But Dr Evans was waiting. Alex took up her position opposite him, beside her instrument table. And beside her, so that their elbows were all but touching, stood Michael. She wondered whether he too was thinking of the fact that they had never worked together before.

Once again she had to force herself to concentrate on her job, and that included watching every move of her nurses, as she was not yet sure of their capabilities. She held out a bowl for the scout nurse to pour in antiseptic lotion with which Dr Evans would paint the operative site. The nurse was holding the bottle of lotion upside down and Alex could not read the label to check its contents. She looked at the nurse with a tiny shake of her head and a flick of her wrist. The nurse got the message immediately and rotated the bottle quickly, and Alex read 'Betadine antiseptic solution: providine iodine 10%', before looking up and catching the nurse's eye. Seeing her flush with embarrassment, Alex gave a tiny wink, acknowledging the tension they were all under this morning. Above her mask, the nurse's eyes were grateful.

Alex passed the bowl of lotion and a sponge on long-handled forceps to Dr Evans, who applied the lotion to the patient's skin in ever-widening circles. The patient was draped, Charles held out a hand for a scalpel, and the operation was under way. Alex handed sponges, retractors, instruments. She threaded needles, kept an eye on her nurses and always on what the surgeons were doing, so she could anticipate their needs.

Everything went smoothly. It was a familiar operation which the surgeons could almost have done with their eyes closed. The movements of their hands were relaxed but precise, and they talked as they worked, mostly about what Charles Evans hoped to see and accomplish in the United States.

When Charles had completed the repair of the floor of the inguinal canal, he said, 'Carry on, Mike,' and stepped back a little way from the table, watching as Michael sutured the external oblique aponeurosis with a continuous running suture.

When it came time for him to suture the skin, Alex allowed herself a small smile behind her mask. Charles's handing over to Michael to close the wound was not just a courtesy, but also a chance for him to assess Michael's ability as a surgeon, to a limited extent. Alex knew Michael would pass the test with flying colours—his 'invisible stitching' had been a byword back in Sydney.

Everyone around the table watched, absorbed, until the last fine stitch was in place. Then, as Michael dropped the needle-holder and scissors into the kidney dish Alex held out to him, Charles said enthusiastically, 'Well done, Mike! Well done, indeed!'

Alex found herself joining in the general murmur of

approval. Standing as close to her as he was, Michael could not fail to hear her. He looked at her quizzically and murmured, 'Thank you.' She lowered her head and became absorbed in sorting the instruments on her trolley. He had deserved his accolade, but she wished he had not heard hers.

The doctors helped transfer the patient on to the trolley, then peeled off caps and masks as the trolley was wheeled away to the recovery-room.

Dr Evans said, 'You're very handy with a needle, Michael.'

Michael demurred, then turned to Alex and asked, with a disarming smile, 'Do you do any needlework, Sister. . .er. . . McLachlan?'

She knew that he was thinking about those rare nights they had had together, before things started to go bad for them, when she would sit quietly working at a piece of tapestry while he read or studied. Eventually he would look up at her, grin and say, 'Ready for bed, Princess?'

She was piqued that she could not stop herself flushing before replying, steadily enough, 'I do a little—when I have time.'

She saw the corner of his mouth twitch. Then he said, 'This is a superb operating unit. Did you have a hand in setting it up?'

'Sister Powers and I spent last week working on it.'

Charles and the anaesthetist were standing, listening, waiting for Michael to leave the theatre with them. But he lingered to ask, 'Have you ever been up this way before, Sister?'

'Yes. But not to work.'

He looked surprised at that, as she had intended he should. She had spent holidays in the Whitsunday area, sailing, in her idle rich days, of which he knew nothing.

'And are you living in town, or in the staff quarters?'

It was the kind of courteous question a doctor might put to a staff member while they were making idle conversation. But it wasn't just idle curiosity that had prompted his enquiry. If they had been alone Alex would have told him it was none of his business where she was living. But they were not alone, so, for the benefit of those listening, she had to reply, albeit tersely, 'I live in the nurses' quarters.'

Since the staff quarters comprised several separate buildings, which they called 'chalets', her answer was not too specific. All the same, there was a note of satisfaction in Michael's voice as he said blandly, 'That's nice.'

She shot him a look, said, 'Will you excuse me, please!' and swung her trolley past him and out of the room.

In the ante-room, she stripped off her surgical gloves furiously, pulled on a pair of thick plastic ones, turned the tap on full and began washing instruments as though they were the objects of her displeasure.

The operation had not been a lengthy one, but she felt as exhausted as if she had just completed a long, full surgical list.

For the next two days, the workload in OR was light and undemanding. Alex could have wished for the pace to have been hectic enough to take her mind off her problems. Michael had one or two procedures, but they fell in Fran's shifts. At least once each day he appeared in OR while Alex was on duty, for some reason—to check up on a booking or an item of paperwork. But he greeted everyone pleasantly and was as impersonal towards Alex as towards the rest of the staff.

On Thursday she met David.

*　*　*

He was tall, fair-haired and very good-looking. And he was feeding a coin into the expired parking meter beside Alex's car.

He looked up and grinned sheepishly as she approached.

'Caught in the act,' he said.

Alex smiled back. 'Thank you. Do you make a habit of frustrating meter maids?'

'No,' he said. 'I don't recall ever having done it before. Pure impulse, I guess. Perhaps it was because your car looks so very feminine and vir. . .er. . .pristine.'

She laughed. 'She *is* practically new,' she admitted, fondly patting the bonnet of her pale blue Honda Accord. Then she added, 'I'm glad to know the age of chivalry isn't dead.'

He sketched a courtly bow and said, 'It would be a pity to waste the rest of the time on the meter now. Would you join me in a drink while it ticks away?'

After his good deed on her behalf, it would be ungracious to refuse. He had an English accent and was probably a tourist, so a little Aussie friendliness seemed called for.

'Why not?' she smiled. 'Could we make it coffee?'

'Certainly.'

They walked a little way up the street, to a coffee lounge with a leafy courtyard. Inside, they found seats surrounded by lush indoor plants. A waitress came and took their order.

Alex sighed gratefully. 'It's so good to sit down. My feet are killing me! If I hadn't had some shopping to do I'd have stayed home and given them a Radox bath.'

'But your shopping was too important?' He looked with a quizzical smile at the almost empty plastic bag she had placed on the table beside her.

'Nylons!' she said succinctly.

'Oh? I thought females in this part of the world never wore such things.'

'They don't. But we still have to, on duty.'

'On duty?'

'Yes. I'm a nurse. In fact, I've just returned to nursing after three months away, and my feet don't seem to have got the message yet that the easy life is over.'

'And you live at the hospital?'

When Michael had asked her that same question a few days ago, it had aroused all kinds of feelings in her. That was why she hesitated now before replying, reminding herself that it did not matter to this man where she lived. He was merely making polite conversation.

'Yes, I live in at the hospital.'

If he had noticed her hesitation, he gave no sign, but said, 'As you've probably guessed, I'm English. I've been in Brisbane for a conference—on marine biology. Being so near, I thought I'd see your Great Barrier Reef before I go home. It's not directly related to my area of research, but the opportunity to see it was too good to miss. By the way, my name is David—David Bartel.'

'And I'm Alex Jones.' She stopped, appalled at how easily that had slipped from her lips. 'Correction,' she said lightly. 'Make that Alex McLachlan.'

He looked at her keenly and a slight flush mounted her cheeks.

'Recently married?' he asked.

'No—the reverse, in fact.'

'Oh, I see! I'm sorry!'

'That's OK.'

At that moment their coffee came. He began talking about his impressions of Queensland, and Alex was grateful that he did not ask any more questions.

Before she knew it, time had slipped away. She looked at her watch and pushed away her empty cup. 'If we don't go, your good deed will have been in vain.'

Indeed, as they left the coffee lounge and turned to walk back to her car, they could see a meter maid standing in front of it, her eyes on the number plate, her pen poised above her pad.

Alex would have accepted the ticket, but David had other ideas. He smiled at the girl and said blithely, 'Hello there!'

The girl said, 'Hello,' and hesitated, her pen still hovering.

'That's an attractive uniform you girls have,' David went on. His look suggested it wasn't only the uniform he found attractive. Alex watched, amused.

The girl's face relaxed at the sound of David's voice. She closed her book and smiled back at him cheekily, letting him know that she was fully aware of the tactics he was using to thwart the course of justice.

'It's your Pommie accent that saved you,' she told him, 'not your sweet-talk. It's the Council's policy to be kind to tourists. Have a nice stay.'

Alex laughed as the girl walked away. 'Now don't tell me it's the first time you've done *that*,' she said.

He grinned, trying to look abashed but not quite succeeding. 'These little challenges help to brighten one's day.'

Alex took her keys from her bag and unlocked the car door.

'Speaking of tomorrow. . .' David said.

'Were we?'

He ignored the interruption and continued, 'Dare I hope that meter maids are not the only ones in this part of the world with a policy of being kind to tourists?'

She laughed. 'I really haven't been here long enough myself to know. Now I must go, before that lass comes back and discovers that this car doesn't belong to a smooth-talking Englishman after all.'

He heid the door for her, then closed it behind her. Alex was glad he didn't follow up on his previous remark. She smiled at him through the window and pulled carefully out from the kerb. Before driving away she glanced back. He was standing in the same spot, watching her. She raised a hand in salute and drove on.

As she drove the short distance to the hospital, she realised she was feeling more light-hearted than she had for a long time. Perhaps she should have let him ask to see her again.

She chuckled. An enterprising young man, as he had shown himself to be, would find a way to see a girl again. If he really wanted to.

CHAPTER FOUR

A HORROR smash on the Bruce Highway next morning kept Alex too busy all day to think about David Bartel, or anything except the emergency treatment of the accident victims the ambulances ferried to the hospital.

A semi-trailer had side-swiped a bus loaded with tourists. The bus had run off the road and overturned, wrapping itself around a tree in the process. Several people, including the driver, were dead. The worst of the injured were being taken to the Mackay Base Hospital and the new Community Hospital had been asked to accept a quota of the remainder.

It was the hospital's baptism of fire, but they were to learn more that day about one another's capabilities and the strengths and weaknesses of their OR organisation than they would have in weeks of normal procedures.

Since only about one third of the hospital's beds were occupied as yet, there were plenty of staff to cope with the influx of emergency patients. The theatre staff was augmented so that both the 'large' and the 'small' theatres could be used simultaneously. The director of nursing herself was taking charge as the patients arrived in Outpatients, deciding which needed the most immediate care, which could safely wait or have minor injuries treated in Outpatients, or be admitted to the wards for observation.

Alex was also pleased to realise, as the day went on, that she had not lost the ability to be calm under pressure, during the months she had not been working.

It wasn't something she regarded as an achievement—she had been that way from the beginning of her training. In a crisis her mind seemed to slip into overdrive, blocking out anything extraneous and becoming crystal-clear, and her hand rock-steady.

When the DON rang through to warn the theatre staff to expect emergency patients, the OR was already set up, waiting for an elderly patient who was scheduled to have a prostatectomy under spinal anaesthesia. The ward was told to hold him indefinitely, and Alex issued a series of crisp orders to her own nurses and to the extra staff who had been sent from the wards to assist.

Michael was to have done the prostatectomy, and he was already in the surgeons' change-room. He went immediately to Outpatients and returned to OR before long, indicating that he and Alex should begin to scrub. While they did, he told her what to expect.

'It's a middle-aged man with internal haemorrhage—probably a ruptured spleen. Multiple lacerations as well, but they'll have to wait.'

'Is he conscious?' asked Alex.

'Fortunately. And quite lucid—no sign of head injury.'

'Has he eaten?'

'Again fortunately, he says he never eats breakfast.'

'Instruments as usual?'

'Yes. Any problem there?' asked Michael.

'No. I'll use the autoclaved emergency set. Will you have an assistant?' she continued.

'Doug should be here any minute—here he is now.'

Doug Weston wasted no time turning on a tap and beginning to scrub.

Alex and Michael left him to it and went through to theatre. As Alex began transferring instruments from the pack a nurse had opened for her, she could hear the anaesthetist talking to the patient, calmly, reassuringly.

'Can you make a fist for me? Great! Now open and shut. Just a little prick. We'll get some blood first and then give you something to make you feel drowsy.'

He inserted a needle into the man's forearm vein, aspirated some blood—for grouping and matching, Alex knew—then injected Pentothal. A few seconds later the man gave one loud snore and the anaesthetist said, 'He's away, Mike.'

The scout nurse removed the covers from the patient, who was then prepped and draped and the operation was under way.

There was no irrelevant conversation this morning. Just the anaesthetist's voice reporting vital signs and Michael's, saying, 'Retractor. . . Sponge. . . Haemostat. . . Suction—stat!'

Then the anaesthetist again. 'His pressure's dropping!'

'Fast?'

'Too fast for my liking!'

'What is it?'

'Fifty on nothing much!'

'Hell! Hang in there, mate. I'll be as quick as I can.'

'Big sucker. And fast!'

It seemed as though everyone in the room held their breath until Michael said, 'Right! I think that's got it. He should begin to stabilise now.'

Another eternity seemed to elapse before the anaesthetist said, 'BP's rising slowly. Pulse is better too. Phew! That was too close for comfort.'

It was not long before the patient, minus his spleen and trailing tubes, was taken to recovery, with the anaesthetist in close attendance. Michael departed to see what the DON had lined up for them next. A team of nurses descended on the theatre, stripping and cleaning it. Alex cleaned her instruments and dropped them into one of the bubbling sterilisers. That was barely done before she was scrubbing for the next case.

And so it went on throughout the day. Mostly she found herself working with Michael, and they made a smooth, efficient team. Once or twice her path crossed that of Fran who had been called on duty and they exchanged quick notes. She made sure that all her nurses had at least one coffee break, but lunch was a non-event.

The cases became progressively less critical as the day went on, but the more minor the procedures the quicker the turnover and the more cleaning and setting-up and scrubbing had to be done. Alex wondered how long it would take her hands to recover.

She lost count of the number of lacerations the surgeons stitched. And the fractures they reduced. One man had his jaw wired to immobilise a fractured mandible. Another had a digital block to repair torn fingers.

Everyone relaxed as the day went on. A little too much, Alex thought, when Michael, off guard, almost let slip the fact that he and Alex had known one another in a past life.

He had been working on a seventeen-year-old girl with facial trauma and had been concentrating hard for some time, in an effort to make the end result for the girl as aesthetically acceptable as possible. She also had a head wound, which had been covered by a large pack.

As Michael neared the end of his work on the face, Alex removed the pack from the girl's head and, surprised, asked whether the head should not have been shaved. The girl had lovely hair, fine, blonde and straight.

'No,' said Michael. 'I told them not to shave. It's a clean cut and will heal nicely if I just tie the hair.'

'Tie the hair?' she repeated.

'Yes. Haven't you seen that done before?'

'As a matter of fact, no.'

'Fair enough,' said Michael. 'I guess those years you spent in obstets left one or two gaps in your surgical experience. I always did. . .'

He stopped as Alex coughed warningly, then looked appalled as he realised how nearly he had given away their secret. They both turned their heads quickly to see who else might have heard, which, if anyone had been watching, would have compounded the felony. Fortunately, the only other person in the theatre was a nurse who was replacing some sterile packs on a table and obviously was not taking any notice of anything else.

Michael and Alex exchanged a relieved glance over the patient's head.

Michael went on to demonstrate how the head wound could be closed, quickly and cleanly, by tying together strands of hair from opposite sides of the cut.

Later, when both the nurse and the patient had departed, and after a careful look round to make sure they were in fact alone, he said, 'A close one, that! Am I forgiven?'

He had stripped off his gloves and pulled down his mask. He wore a rueful, apologetic grin, and Alex couldn't help smiling back.

'There was no harm done. And it has been a long day.'

'I agree,' he said. Then, encouraged by her forgiveness, he added, 'Am I allowed to say that I've enjoyed working with you today?'

'Thank you. And likewise.'

'In fact, I reckon we make a great team!'

She knew he wasn't referring only to their work in surgery now. She turned away, saying nothing, and began to arrange the tiny needles he had used, side by side on her tray.

Friday was another busy day. The operations which had been deferred yesterday to make way for the emergencies were rescheduled for today. But they had to be put back again to make way for one of the accident patients who had been under observation with head injuries and now required urgent surgery for a subdural haematoma.

Alex was very thankful when the time came to hand over to Fran and go off duty. She put her feet up until teatime, then, after tea, decided to go for a walk along the beach. After so many hours standing in one position beside the operating table, and breathing the controlled atmosphere in theatre, she needed fresh air and exercise.

She showered and put on white shorts and an oversized red windcheater, with white sneakers. Through her window she could see the sun sparkling on the water in the distance, so she perched a pair of big white-rimmed sunglasses on top of her hair.

As she crossed the lawn in front of the chalets she could see a man—a fair-haired man—perched on the low wall that marked the hospital boundary. Even though his back was towards her she had no difficulty recognising David Bartel and was somehow not surprised to see him there. He turned as she approached, smiled and stood up.

'Hello again!' he said.

'Hi! What are you doing here?'

'Waiting for you. I hope you don't mind?'

'I don't mind. But you might have sat on that fence

for a long time. I don't always go for a walk in the evening.'

It crossed her mind that he might even have sat there last evening, but she refrained from asking him whether that was so.

'I was admiring the view.' He swept an arm to embrace lush green tropical foliage, brilliant splashes of purple and pink bougainvillaeas and, beyond that, the blueness of sea and sky. 'Actually,' he went on, 'if you hadn't appeared soon, I would have rung the doorbell and asked for you.'

Alex glanced back at the row of chalets visible through the trees and raised her eyebrows. He interpreted her look and said, 'I confess I *did* make enquiries about where you live. I phoned the hospital and got to speak to a lady who said you'd gone off duty. That seemed to be as much as she wanted to say—in fact, she appeared to have a problem believing I was a genuine tourist and not someone assuming a phoney English accent. I eventually convinced her I was the real thing, and she told me where I could find you.'

Alex chuckled. So Fran had been protecting her interests in her absence! And she had summed Michael up pretty accurately. A phoney English accent was just what he would resort to to disguise his identity.

David was looking at her. 'Share the joke?'

She shook her head and waited for him to say something. But he seemed quite content to stand there and look at her. Flushing slightly, she said, 'And after you'd rung the doorbell, what then?'

He looked blank for a moment. 'The doorbell? Oh, of course! I'd have said, "May I speak to Miss Alex McLachlan, please?"'

She laughed. 'And then?' she prompted.

It was his turn to laugh. 'I see what you're getting at! When you appeared, I'd have said, "Miss Alex McLachlan, it's a lovely evening. Would you care to walk on the beach with me?"'

'Now we're getting somewhere! I was fairly sure, of course, you weren't about to ask me out to dinner.' Alex eyed the shorts and T-shirt he was wearing.

She was about to say yes, she would like to walk with him, when she had a sudden, overwhelming desire that it were Michael standing there, smiling at her, without any hideous problems and misunderstandings, between them. But Michael wasn't here. He hadn't even made any real attempt to contact her, even though he had found out where she was living. Irrational though it might be, that hurt.

After a moment, David said quietly, 'I might not be a doctor, but I think I know what to prescribe for you just now.'

'Oh? And what's that?'

'Some male company and a dose of good old-fashioned masculine admiration.'

He was very intuitive—too much so. She must try, in future, not to wear her heart on her sleeve when he was around. She tried to say lightly, 'But you don't know me—I mightn't be. . .admirable.' But to her dismay, her voice trembled and she had to stop and bite her lip. So much for good resolutions!

David said firmly, 'I admire what I see, and that's good enough for me.'

'Then let's walk. But no amateur psychoanalysis, please.'

'I promise.'

She pretended not to see the hand he held out to her as they started off towards the foreshore. When they

reached the beach and began to plough through the still
warm, dry sand towards the water, Alex stopped to kick
off her sandals and, again, David reached for her hand
to steady her. Again she ignored it and ran the last few
yards to the water, laughing as her feet encountered its
delicious coolness.

She turned and looked back to where David was
standing. He was watching her and the look in his eyes
was intense and disturbing. But all he said was, casually,
'Does that feel better?'

She nodded and began to walk along the water's edge.
He fell in beside her and they walked for some minutes
in silence, their feet now splashing in the clear cold
water, or leaving footprints in the wet sand as it receded.
The beach was almost deserted.

Alex sighed contentedly and said, 'It's a lovely evening
for a walk.'

'It's not only the evening that's lovely.' There was a
depth of meaning in his voice that Alex could not
mistake.

It was at that moment she saw, and recognised
instantly, a solitary figure walking towards them. He was
a little higher up the beach and with each step his feet
scuffed up little puffs of dry sand. His head was bent
and his hands were deep in the pockets of his jeans.

Memory struck Alex, like a cold slap in the face.
Those battered blue jeans! She had tried, over and over,
to persuade Michael to throw them away. And the dark
blue floppy sweater—she had given him that for his
birthday last year.

Her reaction against the feelings that were threatening
to overwhelm her was to turn to David, laughingly
accepting the compliment he had just paid her and
holding out her hand to him. He looked surprised, but

only for a second. Then he took her hand, squeezed it and smiled down happily at her.

So, by the time Michael raised his head and saw them, they were swinging along hand in hand, laughing together, two beautiful young people without a care in the world, obviously delighted with one another.

Michael said, 'Hi, there,' as he came level with them.

David replied, 'Lovely evening!' and looked as though he meant it.

Alex caught Michael's eye momentarily as they passed, but could see nothing in his expression that would not have been there had they been just strangers passing one another in the course of an evening stroll. She had to admit he was playing their game extremely well, but, irrationally, she felt disappointed and annoyed with him.

And she had to spend the next half-hour convincing David that holding hands was as far as she was prepared to go with him.

'David, I really like you,' she told him. 'It's just that. . . Oh, what's the use!'

She stood still in desperation and they faced each other.

'I could really do without this conversation just now,' she pleaded. 'I was enjoying our walk. Can't we just carry on with that?'

David was, understandably enough, looking puzzled and stubborn, refusing to accept that she wasn't the tiniest bit interested in him. After all, even though she had started by holding him at arm's length, she had taken his hand and given him reason to hope for something more.

Alex was hoping he would not connect her change of manner with seeing Michael on the beach. There was no reason why he should, but he had shown himself to be unusually perceptive once or twice.

She began to walk again and, to get them over this awkward interlude, asked, 'How long are you staying in Mackay?'

'Oh, that's completely negotiable,' David told her.

'It depends on your company?'

'On my present company.'

Alex refused to rise to that bait, but asked, 'Are you answerable to anyone, or can you stay as long as you like?'

'I have to account for my time. But I've only to say I want to do some research on. . .whatever. . .' he waved an arm '. . .say, on the greenhouse effect as it relates to the Great Barrier Reef, and I could stay indefinitely. You wouldn't want it on your conscience that you'd deprived posterity of the results of that research by not allowing me to stay, would you?'

'I'd take my chance on that. I just don't want you to stay because you have any mistaken ideas about. . .me. I'm just not. . .' Alex had been about to say 'free', but substituted, 'I'm not in the moood for anything remotely resembling romance at present.'

'How would you feel about "just friends", then?'

Her shrug reflected the despondency she had been feeling since seeing Michael on the beach. 'Friends talk,' she said, 'and I can't talk about. . .things. . .not yet.'

'Mates, then?' he persisted. 'A mate who doesn't need to know about. . .things?'

Her eyes misted over. David really was kind. And just having him round was reassuring. As long as he understood the restrictions, why shouldn't they see each other again, if that was what he wanted? She wouldn't give him carte blanche as far as the length of his stay went—just a day at a time.

'Thanks, David,' she said. 'I guess I could use a mate right now. I'm off duty tomorrow. If you like we could play tourists and do some sightseeing.'

His face brightened. 'Great! Where do you suggest?'

They had stopped walking and were sitting on the sand. There was a sprinkling of people at this end of the beach, some sitting, some walking, a few splashing at the water's edge. Further out, several small yachts were skimming before the breeze and, beyond them, away to their left, a big white catamaran was heading up the passage.

Alex pointed at the catamaran and said, 'That's the *Spirit of Roylen* coming in. We could do a day cruise on her.'

'Uh-huh.' David did not seem over-enthusiastic. 'How many passengers does she carry?'

'About three hundred.'

He winced. 'That's what I thought. Does it appeal to you as a way to spend your day off?'

'Not particularly. Do you sail?'

'I've only tried once in my life and that was on Sydney Harbour, a couple of weeks ago. I spent the afternoon dodging the Manly ferry and nearly ended up running aground on one of the islands. . ."doing a Dennis Conner," I think they called it when I told my friends about it.'

She laughed. 'It sounds as though you need some lessons! Would you risk life and limb with me?'

'Darling, I'd risk life and limb with you anywhere,' he said, then added quickly, 'Sorry, mate—won't happen again. Yes, thank you, I would very much like to go sailing with you.'

'You're very trusting,' smiled Alex. 'You haven't so much as asked me whether I *can* sail.'

'I rather took that for granted—Cap'n.'

'Good! A captain needs to have the confidence of her crew. Now, let me think. Where shall we go?. . . Airlie Beach, I think. It's up the coast, about an hour and a half's drive on the main highway. We could pick up some food in Airlie, hire a boat in Shute Harbour, and go find ourselves an island.'

'A deserted one?' David asked hopefully, then added quickly, 'All right—not too deserted!'

Alex ignored the interruption and proceeded, 'We'll need to book a boat. . .'

'Can I do that?' he offered.

'I think I'd better, seeing I talk the language. You have to pass a sailing test before the charterers will trust you with a bareboat.'

'A bare boat? Sounds a bit Spartan!'

She chuckled. 'Anything but! A bareboat simply means sail-it-yourself. They're extremely well equipped.'

'I see. And the sailing test?'

'Oh, that's usually just a couple of tacks, a gybe and throwing a reef in the main. Nothing to worry about.'

'And will I know how to do all those things by the end of the day?'

'That and much more, I hope. Is seven-thirty too early to start? If you tell me where you're staying I'll pick you up there.'

Alex stood up and brushed the sand from her legs. David did likewise and they began the walk back to the hospital. When they reached the spot where they had met earlier, she stopped.

'I'll be fine from here,' she told him.

'You sure?'

'Yes, of course. I'll see you tomorrow.'

It was almost dark. He placed both hands on her shoulders and stood looking down at her. In spite of his earlier assurances, she knew by the look in his eyes that she had only to raise her face a fraction and mateship would take wings. She was tempted, but recognised, in time, her motivation for what it really was—the need to be close to someone, to know that she was still attractive to a man, and a very handsome man at that. But he would read too much into it and would probably stay around, hoping for something she could not give him.

So she remained still and unresponsive under his hands. He gave a tiny sigh, then stooped and placed a gentle kiss on her forehead.

'See you in the morning. . .mate.'

'Goodnight, David.'

'Goodnight.'

When Michael saw Alex walking on the beach that evening with a strange man, his instincts were pure caveman. He wanted to deck the guy, grab Alex by force and leave no doubt in anyone's mind, including hers, that he had first claim on her.

After the day they had had in OR, he had decided to go for a walk to get the kinks out of his back and the circulation going in his legs. Someone else had taken charge of the accident patients who had been admitted and he, Mike, would only be called if there was another flap on.

So he'd walked and inevitably, after spending all day working with her, he had thought about Ally.

It was six days now, since he had come to Mackay and found her here ahead of him. He had put his career on hold, with some difficulty, because he had known he had to get away from Sydney, where everyone and everything reminded him of Ally. People had been kind, but of course they had been curious, and how could you answer their questions when you couldn't answer your own? He had decided he had to stop looking for answers he was never likely to get and make long-term, objective decisions about his future as a single man.

But it had been out of the frying pan, into the fire!

All his old feelings of resentment and betrayal had flared up, worse than ever, on seeing her again. And in OR, where there was no possible chance of avoiding her. His spur-of-the-moment suggestion that they carry on as though they were strangers had been made on the assumption that they wouldn't have to see all that much of one another. He hadn't known then that she would be working in OR where they couldn't hope to avoid one another. Anyway, the strangers idea had, at least, given them both time to get their heads on straight before the inevitable confrontation.

He knew that Ally had been as shocked at seeing him as he was, seeing her. He admitted that, as a result of feeling as he had, he had been a bit hard on her at the party. But the way she had turned the tables on him so neatly the next day indicated that she could cope. He writhed in mental anguish still at the thought of those awful moments at the end of the hospital tour, when she had walked away with her head in the air and he'd been left trying to explain to five rather sceptical old people that he had merely been playing a prank on Sister—'the kind of rag that medical students get up to now and then'. The old folk had gone off looking unconvinced. They'd probably dine out on the story for weeks, and Charles would come back to a decimated practice in a couple of months' time! But he had to admire Ally's spunk.

Once he had decided to let things settle down for a while and not force any issues with her just yet, he found that his emotions were more under control, though they were still, at times, a confused medley of resentment and desire, with resentment fading and desire increasing every time he saw her, looking beautiful and aloof, at work.

Like tonight, as he walked along the beach, desire was definitely uppermost in his mind. He had so many memories to fuel desire. And he was so confident, now, that they would eventually work things out that he was actually visualising her here, walking by his side, laughing as they'd used to do, at anything or nothing. There were boats on the water, skimming along before the breeze. He was fantasising about sailing away with her to some remote tropical island. . .

And then he saw her!

She was walking towards him, her hair blown into a tousled dark nimbus about her face. Her legs were long and bare and golden beneath brief white shorts. She was so lovely, so desirable.

And she was hand in hand with another man! What was more, they were laughing together, just as he, so short a time ago, had been imagining he and she would do. To make matters worse, the guy, whoever he was, was a veritable Adonis, tall, fair-haired and impossibly handsome.

It was almost more than Mike could manage not to step into their path and ask the fellow what he meant by messing about with another man's wife.

What he did do, being civilised, was to twist his mouth

into the nearest thing he could manage to a smile, and
say, 'Hello there!' as they passed.

'Hi! Lovely evening!' the man replied cordially.

The smug, self-satisfied jerk!

Mike's hands tightened into fists and he thrust them
deep into the pockets of his jeans. He didn't look back
after they had passed. But Ally's face remained with
him, relaxed and laughing and not at all disconcerted
that he had seen her in the company of another man.

So who *was* the man? Mike knew he would have no
peace of mind until he found out. And probably even
less once he did!

Was he a local? He hadn't been at either of the hospital
shindigs, so he probably wasn't a doctor.

How long had Ally known him? Had she—Mike's jaw
tightened at the thought—come up here to be with him?
The idea did absolutely nothing for Mike's now defunct
peace of mind. Had something been going on between
them for goodness knew how long? Was he the reason
she had walked out on him? He rejected that idea out of
hand at first, telling himself that he would have known
if anything like that had been going on. But would he?
He had to admit that, after the first few months of idyllic
married life, he had come to take Ally pretty much for
granted. He'd been so engrossed in his study and his
work, assuming that she'd be there on the increasingly
rare occasions when he surfaced for brief intervals—
when he needed her, her sympathy, her laughter, her
loving.

He groaned. He needed her now, needed desperately
to know that this man, whoever he was, didn't really
count for anything—that there was still hope of a future
together with Ally again.

Then he remembered something else that didn't do

much for his peace of mind. That day in theatre, when he had asked her, just for a joke, whether she had ever been up this way before. He was so sure she hadn't that her reply had quite floored him. Now he wondered whether the truth of it was that she had come up here during those months when she had vanished and he hadn't been able to find her. Had she met this fellow and something had started between them then?

Mike returned to his quarters with his mind in turmoil.

He was living in the Evans's home, in a suite of rooms occupied, when he was home, by their son Martin, who had recently qualified in ENT.

Ellen, Charles's wife, was a pleasant soul with a highly developed maternal instinct, who was inclined to knock on Mike's door rather too often, offering him cups of tea, or looking for a friendly chat. Fortunately, as a doctor's wife, she had a great deal of respect for a doctor's reading, and Mike had realised that he only had to appear with a few medical journals under his arm and announce that he had some study to do and he would be left in peace.

Tonight he was feeling anything but sociable, but he dropped into their sitting-room to find out whether Charles had received any further reports on the accident victims. He had not, so Mike chatted for a few minutes, refused Ellen's offer of iced tea and excused himself, saying he had some notes to look up. He was sitting in his big armchair when there was a knock on the door and Charles's voice said, 'Y'there, Mike?'

Mike grabbed a book, opened it at random and called, 'Come in!'

'Sorry to interrupt,' said Charles.

'No problem. Take a seat.'

'Ellen and I have been talking, Mike. Once I fly out on Sunday, it won't be easy for you to get away. You've done a great job for the last couple of days, and the practice is well covered tomorrow. Why don't you take a free day and do some sightseeing?'

'That's kind of you,' said Mike, 'but I don't really. . .'

'Now, no arguing! It'll do you good. And Ellen will be most disappointed if you don't go. She's already planning a picnic lunch for you to take along.'

Mike felt singularly unenthusiastic about sightseeing. But two things occurred to him. As it was Charles's last day before he left, Charles and Ellen just might like some time on their own. And to his certain knowledge Ally had not had a day off this week. There was a good chance she could be free tomorrow. And if so, she just might consider spending some of it with him. It was worth a try. She could only say no. Of course, that other chap might have designs on her free day, but why should he, Mike, sit back and let him have things all his own way? He could at least ring her. Even if she wasn't free tomorrow, he might find out who the man was.

He said, 'OK, Charles, I'll take you up on your offer. And thanks to you both.'

'That's great! Ellen said to take her car. There are maps in the glove compartment. Do you have any idea where you'll go?'

'None whatever. Any suggestions?'

'Well. . .southwards, the beaches around Sarina are lovely. Inland is Eungella National Park—sugar cane country and rain forest. North is Airlie Beach—a couple of hours' drive, but well worth it.'

'It's going to be hard to decide,' said Mike. 'I think I'll leave my options open till I study the maps in the morning.'

And ring Ally, he thought. What he did tomorrow would depend entirely on Ally.

Charles said goodnight and departed. Mike sat for several minutes, wondering whether to ring Ally right away. He went so far as to reach out a hand and pick up the receiver. He sat listening to the dial tone for a minute, looking thoughtful. If he rang her now, it would look like a knee-jerk reaction after seeing her on the beach with that man. Better not to rush it. He replaced the receiver.

Then anger surged in him as he realised that Ally and the man might be together still. They could be anywhere, enjoying themselves, while he, Mike, sat chewing his nails to the quick—metaphorically, of course. Even *in extremis* a surgeon had to be meticulously careful about his hands.

He stood up and paced the room. It was incredible— the idea of another man in Ally's life! Since that night when they had met at the hospital dance and fallen headlong in love, it had been just Ally and himself. No one else! Not for him. Not for her. Everyone who knew them knew that. From then on it had been Alex and Mike. Forever, he had believed.

And now?

He came to a halt in front of the telephone. His hand went out, but he drew it back. He was too uptight to talk to her now. If he went ape, she might clam up and refuse to see him at all. Or even run away again. Better wait until morning and hope he had simmered down by then.

Nice and steady, he advised himself. That was the only way to go.

CHAPTER FIVE

ALEX woke next morning with a sense of pleasurable anticipation, rather than of excitement. That was the effect David had on her—a comfortable warmth, not fire. There had been no fire for her since the last night she and Michael had spent together.

She lay with her eyes closed, thinking about her marriage and how she would wake up in the morning, in those early months, and look at Michael sleeping beside her and wonder at the fact that he loved her as much as she loved him. And even when she had begun to doubt that, the fire had still been there and it had taken so little to ignite it—a word, a look, a touch. . .

She turned restlessly over in bed and a shaft of sunlight pierced her closed lids, bringing her back to reality. She was going sailing today, with David, and she was determined to enjoy herself. The weatherman had predicted a warm day, not as hot as yesterday, but good for sailing.

She showered, slipped on her soft white terry-towelling gown and sat down at her dressing-table to apply some careful skin protection. Even when she had been living on a student nurse's pay, she had never economised on skin care. Her days off were almost always spent either in or on the water, swimming or board-surfing at Manly or Bondi, or sailing on the Harbour in whatever boat they could beg or borrow. The sun, the surf and the wind would play havoc with one's complexion if one did not take good care.

The brand names on the bottles on Alex's dressing-table had sometimes caused raised eyebrows and envious whistles from her fellow nurses in those days, but no one really questioned how she could afford them. After all, if a girl wanted to blow a month's pay on expensive make-up, that was her business.

Looking back, as she applied moisturiser and block-out lotion this morning, she wondered whether she had not been naïvely idealistic, even immature, to have made the grand gesture of renouncing her wealth. She wondered, as she had so many times before, what difference it would have made if Michael had known about it from the outset. Which led to the further vexed question—*had* he known?

One thing she did know, and that was that when she had decided not to keep up the pretence any longer she had felt that she had suddenly grown up. Buying her car had been the final step in the change in her lifestyle, and she had arrived in Mackay with a new Honda Accord, a completely refurbished wardrobe and a sigh of relief at no longer having to keep up her deception.

When Fran knocked on her door and came in a little later, Alex was dressed in black linen shorts and a Ken Done top, splashed in vivid colour. On the bed lay a broad-brimmed hat with a co-ordinating scarf and sun-glasses to match.

Fran nodded approval. 'Nice—very nice! But it doesn't look quite right for the "nothing much" you said you were going to do on your days off.'

Alex smiled. 'No. Something came up that sounded more interesting.'

'Oh? Not Michael?'

'Definitely not Michael—David.'

'David?' Alex could see Fran searching her mind for a

doctor or male nurse in the hospital named David. 'A doctor?' Fran asked. Then light dawned and her eyes widened. 'Not your tourist?'

'As a matter of fact, yes,' said Alex.

Alex had told Fran about meeting David on Wednesday but had not had a chance to update the story. She did so now, making it sound as though their second meeting had been as much by chance as the first, and playing down David's obvious attraction to her. She told her, briefly, of their plans for today. Then Fran, in uniform and on her breakfast break, suddenly checked her watch and realised that she was going to be late back on duty. She rushed out of the door, calling, 'Make sure you tell me all about it tonight!'

Alex packed some articles into a white, soft leather carry-bag, slipped her feet into well-worn docksiders and was ready to leave. She detoured into the sitting-room near the front door on her way and wrote 'Off duty. Away all day' against her name on the directory board beside the phone.

As she finished, the phone began to ring. She glanced at her watch. It was already seven twenty-five, and she had told David she would call for him at seven-thirty. If she answered the phone and then had to rouse some sleepy nurse to take the call, she would be late. Somewhat guiltily, she decided to ignore the phone and hurried round to the car park at the rear of the chalets.

Mike had decided that seven-thirty was a reasonable time to ring Ally. But by seven twenty-five he was in a fervour of impatience and picked up the phone and began dialling. The ringing tone sounded for some time before a sleepy voice said, 'Hello.' He asked to speak to Alex

McLachlan, having carefully drilled himself not to say 'Jones'. The voice said, 'Hold on.'

He expected to have to wait for a while and began to rehearse, for the umpteenth time, what he would say when Ally answered. But the voice was back almost immediately.

'Sorry, she's out—all day, according to the board. Can I leave a message for her?'

'Thanks. No.' He hung up.

So that was that! He was frustrated and furious, both with himself and with Ally. He had been correct in assuming that she could be off duty today. But he had wrongly surmised she would begin the day by sleeping in. The question that tormented him was, had she gone off somewhere for the day with that man?

His own day seemed not worth worrying about any longer, but he still wanted to get away on his own for the day. And to leave Charles and Ellen to spend their day together.

He went to the kitchen and found Ellen putting the finishing touches to his lunch basket. He managed to greet her cheerfully and say no, he wouldn't stop for breakfast. He was keen to get on the road and would pick up some coffee somewhere before too long.

Charles, hearing voices, appeared with the car keys. Had Michael decided where he would go? No, he'd just follow his fancy for a while. He received his picnic basket from Ellen, said thanks and goodbye and left the house.

He didn't know, and he didn't care, where he was going, but he had turned left out of Charles's driveway, which meant he was heading in a northerly direction. He drove until he had calmed down enough to tell himself he was stupid to feel so angry with Ally. She was free to do what she wanted on her day off. Just so long as she remembered she was still his wife, if she *was* with that man and he had any ideas of getting up to monkey business with her!

Michael crossed a bridge over a river into an area which was a mixture of sugar cane paddocks and new suburbs. He had been this way before, visiting a patient with Charles. He might as well stay on the road he was on—it seemed to be a main highway. He figured he was travelling north-west. A road sign said PROSERPINE 120k. He couldn't remember Charles mentioning Proserpine, but it had a nice ring to it. Perhaps he might get some enjoyment out of his day after all, even without Ally.

With his return to a degree of equanimity, the thought of coffee became enticing, and when he saw a roadhouse he pulled in and took Ellen's road maps from the glove compartment. Over coffee and toast with Vegemite, he studied the maps.

Proserpine was inland. By continuing on eastwards he would come to Airlie Beach and Shute Harbour, which Charles had mentioned. On a warm day like this he preferred to be near the ocean. He folded his map, drained his coffee-cup and spent a minute or two chatting with the girl at the cash register. He had his back to the road. Even had he seen the pale blue Honda Accord go by, he would not have recognised it as Alex's because he didn't even know she owned a car. It was travelling at speed, with David behind the wheel.

Michael went on his way, enjoying the scenery. There was an air of despondency about Proserpine as he drove through it, perhaps reflecting the dramatic fall in the demand for sugar on world markets. He found the road to Airlie Beach and was pleased to be heading towards the coast again.

Airlie Beach was a resort town, bustling with tourists

even at this time of the year. It sported a range of interesting shops and restaurants, and Michael resolved to investigate these on his way back.

Shute Harbour was some way from Airlie, but the drive through tropical countryside was pleasant. The final turn into Shute Harbour brought a surprise. He had assumed, rightly, that Airlie Beach was the main resort town in the area and he had expected Shute Harbour to be something of an anticlimax, perhaps with a wharf, a kiosk and a few tourist boats. He was unprepared for the sight of hundreds of boats jammed into the harbour, ranging from huge luxury catamarans to smaller cruisers and charter yachts. A multi-storey car park, at the base of tall cliffs, was jammed with cars. There was a food shop and a souvenir shop and that was about all. It seemed that sailors in these parts lived in Airlie Beach and commuted to Shute Harbour to their boats.

It was a scene that demanded a photograph—the white boats clustered at the various wharves and scattered across the Harbour, the intense blue of the water of the Whitsunday Passage, the darker blue of islands breaking the horizon. Mike reached for his camera, but remembered it had no film. The souvenir shop on the waterfront displayed a large Kodak sign, so he pulled into the nearest available parking spot and walked into the shop.

'Well, looks like you just missed the boat,' said a suntanned, middle-aged woman behind the counter.

'Sorry?' enquired Mike, and then, noticing through the window an enormous catamaran with 'Hamilton Island' emblazoned on her, he added, 'Oh, I see what you mean. But actually I just came in to buy a roll of film.' He put his camera on the counter and said, '100 ASA if you have it, please.'

The woman chuckled. 'What else? With all this sunshine that's about the only speed we sell.' She turned and selected a roll from the display case behind her. She took the note Mike offered and took change from her till, saying, 'Sure I can't interest you in a cruise to Daydream Island? We've got one leaving in about fifteen minutes—only takes two hours, with lunch on board.'

'Thanks. Another day, perhaps.' Daydream Island. There was magic in the name. If his dreams came true he would take Ally there one day.

He turned to go, but stood back as the door opened and another customer entered. Seen in silhouette against the bright sunlight, the man entering seemed vaguely familiar. It was only as he approached the counter and Mike's eyes adjusted to the light that he realised it was the man he had seen on the beach with Ally last evening.

So! Mike's day had taken an unexpectedly interesting turn. Perhaps he wouldn't have to rely on Ally to tell him who her friend was. Here was an even more direct source of information.

Quickly he turned back into the shop and asked the assistant, who was just about to start serving the new arrival, 'Do you happen to sell camera batteries as well?'

'Sure. Mind if I just serve this customer first?'

Disappointed, Mike thought that his ruse to get into conversation with the man was not going to work. But the other man said pleasantly, 'No, go ahead. First come, first served, after all.'

He spoke with an English accent, not seeming to recognise Michael from the brief exchange on the beach. That gave Mike his opening. As the woman searched in a drawer for the battery he wanted, he turned to the man and said, 'Thanks,' adding, 'You're a tourist? English, by the accent?'

'That's so.'

'Been here long?'

'In Australia? No—three weeks, actually, and most of that in Brisbane. I'm just finishing off with a few days in Mackay.'

'Oh? You have friends in Mackay?' asked Michael.

'No,' the man said, then seemed to change his mind. 'Well, you know how it is on holidays. . .one meets people.'

One picks up people, thought Mike—such as girls walking on a beach. But he suddenly felt as though a heavy weight had been lifted from him and, in a rush of friendly feeling, he held out his hand.

'I'm Michael Jones,' he said. 'I hope you enjoy the rest of your stay in Australia.' Liar, he told himself— that's about the last thing I want. The sooner you take yourself back to the UK, old man, the better I'll be pleased. Not that he didn't seem a decent enough chap— looking a little bit surprised just now at the friendliness of this total stranger, but probably reminding himself that Aussies had a reputation for being outgoing.

He took Michael's extended hand. 'And I'm David Bartel,' he said.

David Bartel—tourist—transient. Here today, gone tomorrow—or so soon as not to matter. And nothing more than a very casual acquaintance of Ally's! That was the marvellous, fantastic truth!

Michael was elated, smugly self-satisfied with the results of his few minutes of sleuthing. He took his battery from the woman, paid her, said, 'Nice to have met you. Have a good trip back,' to David Bartel and walked out of the shop with a spring in his step and a broad smile on his face.

And there, not two metres away, sitting in the passenger seat of a car parked at the kerb right outside the shop, was Ally.

Mike had been so engrossed in his encounter with David Bartel, he had completely overlooked the possibility, which he had previously assumed, that Ally was spending her day off with the man she had met on the beach last evening.

Alex turned her head as the door of the shop opened, clearly expecting to see David Bartel emerging.

Mike and Alex were both momentarily speechless, their surprise mirrored in their faces. Mike hesitated, then crossed the pavement to stand by the car, looking down at Alex.

'Hello,' he said.

'Hello,' she replied.

Another silence. Then they both rushed into speech.

'What are you. . .?'

'Fancy meeting. . .'

They both stopped in mid-sentence and burst out laughing.

At that moment David emerged from the shop, with a large ice-cream in each hand.

'You two know each other, then?' he asked.

'Well, yes, you could say that,' said Mike.

Before he had a chance to add anything, Alex interrupted with, 'This is Michael Jones, a doctor at the hospital where I work. And this is David Bartel,' she said to Mike.

'We did introduce ourselves in the shop,' said David, looking at Michael with interest. When Michael had introduced himself in the shop, the name 'Jones' had not meant anything to David. It was a very common name.

But seeing him here, with Alex, he recalled her introducing herself as 'Alex Jones. . .' before correcting herself.
But, with the way they had been laughing together,
sharing some joke as he had come out of the shop, with
no sign of tension between them, he was inclined to
dismiss it as pure coincidence that this man was called
Jones. He was probably what Alex had said—a doctor at
the hospital where she worked. If he really thought he
was the Jones who had caused Alex so much distress, he
would have been inclined to punch him in the nose,
rather than offer him an ice-cream cone, as he now did,
saying, 'Would you care for one of these? I can duck
back for another one.'

'No, thanks. But go ahead, or they'll melt in this sun.'

David handed Alex one of the cones through the
window and she immediately applied a dainty tongue to
a threatened drip at its edge. David attacked his more
directly, then said to Michael, 'A doctor, huh? On a day
off?'

'Yes. Doing a spot of sightseeing.'

'Your first time up here, then?'

'Yes.'

'Do you sail?'

Mike's eyes flickered towards Alex and caught the
glimmer of a smile on her face.

'Well, yes, I do—a little.'

Alex appeared to choke on a mouthful of ice-cream.
David seemed not to notice but continued, 'We've
booked a boat for the day, but I'm no sailor.' Turning to
Alex, he asked, 'Do you think we should ask him to
come along too? You might feel safer with a competent
crewman on board.'

Ally was not smiling now, observed Mike. He
chuckled inwardly, seeing the fix she was in. She could

not refuse to have him along without appearing discourteous. Yet the last thing she would want would be to have the three of them spend several hours in close proximity on a yacht. After last Sunday she was probably wondering, with justification, what embarrassing prank he might think of, in those circumstances.

All the same, if Mike had not found out what he had about David Bartel, he might have risked Ally's displeasure and accepted David's invitation, whether or not Ally made it a mutual one. But, knowing what he did, he could afford to be magnanimous. And anyway, it wasn't exactly his idea of a fun way to spend a day, watching a complete stranger flirt with his wife under his very nose.

'Thanks, but no, thanks,' he said to David, and was aware of Ally's barely disguised sigh of relief. 'Nice-looking car you've got,' he said to David, in a further attempt at friendliness, to offset his refusal to go sailing. 'I've always said Accords are a great car. I hadn't seen the new model before. . . I'd buy one myself if I could afford it.'

'Oh, it's not mine!' explained David. 'It belongs to Alex.' David felt confirmed in his assumption that this Jones man was a relative stranger to Alex. He certainly didn't appear to know much about her—hadn't even known that she had a car. He was looking surprised— probably wondering how a nurse could afford a car like that on her salary.

Mike was *feeling* surprised. After all, it wasn't much more than three months since he and Ally had been battling to find next month's rent on their apartment. And here she was in a car like this! Oh, well! Perhaps her mother, or grandmother, had forked out for it. *They'd* never seemed short of cash. In fact, he had wondered more than once, since marrying Ally, why they'd never offered to help out a bit financially, but had decided that Ally must have told them he was a bit touchy on the subject of money.

Alex was watching him keenly, as if trying to read what was going through his mind. There was nothing much he could say, except to repeat, 'And very nice it is too! Being so new, you can't have had it long?'

'Not long,' she said shortly.

'Well, I must let you get on with this boating business. It's a good day for it.' He looked, with an expert eye, at white clouds moving across a blue sky at just the rate to please a sailor.

David said, 'If you're sure you won't join us. . .?'

'Quite, thanks.'

David walked around the car and slid in behind the wheel. But Alex suddenly seemed to want to continue talking. Perhaps she felt more comfortable, now that David could not see her face as she looked at Michael through the open window.

'How did you get to Shute?' she asked. 'Do you have a car?'

'Charles told me to take Ellen's car and make myself scarce for the day. He leaves for overseas tomorrow and then according to him, my easy life ends.'

'Are you enjoying. . .being a locum?'

He shrugged. 'It's different. . .more relaxed, less pressure. There's time to get to know the patients.'

'What do you plan to do when you finish in Mackay? Go back to Sydney?'

'Who knows! Anything can happen between now and then. I'll just wait and see what each day brings,' Michael told her.

'You don't find it frustrating—waiting?'

Michael knew what she was talking about—and it wasn't about his work. He suddenly felt impatient with this roundabout conversation, saying one thing and meaning another. He had thought it might be amusing, playing at being strangers with Ally. But he suddenly decided he didn't like it at all. He wanted to get to the bottom of things, know what was what, have everything out in the open. He was heartily fed up with all the mystery and suspense.

'I don't plan to wait too long,' he said in reply to her question, and his voice was serious and convincing. 'Life is meant for living, and I mean to get on with it, one way or the other.'

Alex couldn't mistake his meaning. She continued to look at him steadily, but there was a mistiness in her eyes and a tightening of her lips, as though she was trying to stop them trembling.

'You do that,' she said.

Mike felt like a heel and wished he hadn't hit out at her, just because he had been feeling so frustrated. With a sudden rush of warm protectiveness and a rough edge to his voice to hide his emotion, he said, 'And you take care out in that boat. Keep an eye on those tides. Apparently, in some spots out there, in light winds, you're hard pressed to make any headway against the tide. Nothing like going backwards down the Passage! It's a bit different from Sydney Harbour, remember. 'Bye.'

David Bartel could make what he liked of all that, Mike thought as he walked towards his own car. After all, it was Bartel who was the stranger here. Alex still belonged to him, Mike—as much as one could say a woman belonged to a man in these enlightened, feminist days.

CHAPTER SIX

ALEX passed her sailing test with the charter base people with flying colours.

David too made a reasonable showing, thanks to the half-hour Alex had spent instructing him in the rudiments of sailing, sitting in the car between saying goodbye to Michael and presenting themselves at the base.

David was somewhat amazed at the size of the boat that awaited them, but Alex assured him that it was considerably safer than one of the smaller ones that skimmed about so easily on the Harbour.

At the conclusion of the test, Alex discussed with the base crew their possible destination and accepted their suggestion that she and David make for Cid Harbour, which was a couple of hours' sailing time from Shute and provided a good all-weather anchorage in case of a blow.

The base crew again complimented Alex on her ability, wished them a good day and headed off back to dock in the runabout that had been towed behind the *Ariadne* for the sailing test.

They had cleared the harbour now and the wind was coming from the south-west. Alex told David to take the wheel and steer east by north-east, while she went to ease the boom vang to compensate for the wind.

'And try not to hit the reef off the southern tip of South Molle Island,' she chuckled.

David responded to the challenge and became

absorbed in his task. But once or twice, when he was free to take his eyes from the compass or the seas ahead, she found him watching her speculatively, and she guessed he was trying to make sense of that conversation she had had with Michael. But he didn't say anything, and one or two brief silences were compensated for by the magic of the scenery.

The steady sou'-westerly gave them an easy broad reach across to Cid Island and the much larger Whitsunday Island, the largest in the group.

Time passed idyllically. Alex knew of no better way to forget one's problems than this, and David seemed not to have a care in the world.

The wind died down as they rounded Loriard Point and Alex, remembering Michael's warning about going backwards down the channel, decided it would be wiser to use the diesel to push against the flood tide flowing down Hunt Channel which was slowing the boat to a crawl. She took the wheel and shouted orders to David as he attempted to furl the sails.

Free of that duty, he became so enthusiastic about the beauty of the islands that he perched on the cabin roof to take photographs while Alex nudged the boat into Sawmill Beach on the western side of Whitsunday Island.

'This is magnificent!' he shouted to Alex. 'The mountains, the green water, you. . .'

'The forward hand gets to look after the anchor,' she called back. 'We'll need to let out quite a bit of scope. You'd better grab the lead line from the hatch to see how the water depth is going.'

David had an almost ludicrous look on his face as he tried to make sense of all that nautical lingo.

'What's scope?' he asked. 'Hey! I just saw a turtle swim past.'

Alex laughed. 'Let's concentrate on the job, *then* enjoy the beauties of nature—not to mention lunch!'

David set to with a will, obviously enjoying himself to the full. When Alex was happy that they weren't dragging the anchor, she suggested a short swim off the side of the boat before lunch. Then they settled down on the warm deck to a lunch of cold chicken, salad, and crunchy bread rolls, washed down with a bottle of ice-cold Chardonnay that David had stowed in the ice-box earlier.

'This is a great way to spend a day,' he said contentedly, his eyes following a flock of native parrots that had been disturbed high in the hills above them and flew, squawking raucously, out over the *Ariadne* and back to the shelter of the trees just beyond the beach.

Alex nodded agreement.

'You don't regret not having your doctor friend along?' David asked.

'No, I think we've managed very well without him. You're a quick learner and you do what you're told promptly, which is essential on a boat.'

'I've had a good teacher,' he said, 'although I imagine we've barely scraped the surface of boating lore.'

'You're right. There's always more to learn, for the best of sailors.'

'You sailed a lot in Sydney?' he asked.

'Oh, yes. At every opportunity.'

Memories came flooding back—of days off, of weekends, of mid-week races during long summer evenings of daylight saving. Lovely lazy times, with Michael whenever possible, or with friends, if Michael was working.

'With Michael?'

David asked the question so quietly, and it was so much in tune with her thoughts, that without thinking she nodded her head. Then, with widened eyes and a slight flush mounting her cheeks, she turned to look at him.

'You guessed!'

It was a statement, not a question.

He smiled at her gently. 'It wasn't too difficult, Alex Jones—McLachlan.'

She gave a small rueful smile. 'I did make it easy for you, didn't I? But you caught me off guard.'

'Michael's your husband?'

'Yes.'

'And you're separated?'

'Yes.'

'Not divorced?'

'No. Not yet, at least.'

'And you're still hurting rather badly,' David guessed.

'I thought I was getting over it. But then he turned up, unexpectedly, in Mackay. And now. . .' Alex sighed deeply and her eyes, gazing off into the distance, were troubled, sad.

David too was quiet, not looking at her, but watching a large cruise boat which was stationary, far out on the water. When, after a time, the boat began to move, he stirred and said, still without looking at her, 'All this isn't turning out as I'd expected—hoped. I can't say you didn't warn me. But I can't pretend I'm not disappointed.'

She said nothing and he went on, 'Am I right in thinking that there's nothing to be gained by my staying on in Queensland?'

'I can't see anything to be gained. . .anywhere. It's all just. . .hopeless.' The small break in her voice reflected the emptiness in her heart and she turned her head so that he could not see her face.

He reached a hand and covered hers, where it lay on the sun-warmed deck between them.

'Would it help to talk about it?' he asked.

'I couldn't. . .not now. But thanks. I thought I had it all straight in my mind and I was beginning to get my act together again. But since he came back, everything's confused. . .'

'Can I punch him on the jaw for you?' He said it lightly but with an undertone of grim relish that told her he would derive quite some satisfaction from the act.

She laughed shortly. 'Thanks for the offer! I confess there have been times when I might have taken you up on it. But I guess we'll just be civilised about it all. As yet,' she admitted, 'we haven't even talked.'

'Except in riddles,' David said. 'I suppose that was all for my benefit, back there at Shute Harbour?'

'Only partly. It's all part of the game we're playing. You see, we haven't told anybody in Mackay that we know one another.'

'Really!' he said, surprised. 'How do you manage that?'

'With great difficulty, at times.' Alex could not repress a smile at the thought of what had happened on the Sunday afternoon tour of the hospital.

'Share the joke?' he pleaded.

'Why not?' This was something she *could* tell him. She gave a succinct account of what had happened that day.

He chuckled. 'Well done! That confirms the feeling I had that you can take care of yourself. Did you ever discover how he explained himself to the others in the group?'

'No. Until today, we hadn't spoken about anything that wasn't strictly business. And, speaking of today,' she went on, 'that breeze has been building up for the last hour or so. We should probably get under way.'

She reached for the hamper and began stowing away the considerable amount of food that remained.

'Another drink?' he asked.

'Just a small one.' He poured one for her and for himself and, as they sipped, she began outlining her plans for the afternoon. They still had two or three hours' sailing time. They would potter about for a while, she would give David some more sailing lessons and then they would head back to Shute Harbour.

David agreed, and they moved the boat out into deeper water where Alex began to explain some tactical manoeuvres they had not yet had occasion to use. But it was not long before she sensed a subtle change in David's attitude, and guessed that he had relinquished any idea of prolonging his stay in Australia and would be returning to England without further delay.

When she used the excuse that the wind seemed to be getting up and it might be wise to set course for Shute Harbour without further ado, he agreed so readily that her suspicions were confirmed.

They would have a meal in Airlie, drive back to Mackay, say goodbye, and that would be that. All neat and tidy. Just a pleasant interlude to look back on for a while and then forget about.

But it was not to be quite like that.

Alex had gone below to check that their gear was stowed securely, when the radio in the cabin crackled into life.

'I'll get that!' she called.

'*Ariadne*, this is Whitsunday Charters. Do you read? Over.'

'Whitsunday Charters, this is *Ariadne*. Over.'

'Good afternoon—Alex, isn't it? Sorry to do this to you, but we've got a bit of a blow building up to south of you. Some of our yachts down around the Shaw Islands have been taking quite a buffeting. Can you give us your exact position?'

'We've just left Sawmill Beach, heading north around Cid Island,' said Alex.

'Glad we caught you before you left Cid Harbour. It's a different story out in the Passage. Our suggestion is that you head back into Sawmill Bay, rather than Sawmill Beach, and tuck in behind the reef. That should give you plenty of protection.'

'Certainly, Whitsunday Charters,' replied Alex. 'We'll head into Sawmill Bay now.'

'Thank you, *Ariadne*. Could you please radio in when you're securely anchored? It should blow over during the night, so you'll be able to head back in at first light. Have a good night. Whitsunday Charters clear.'

Alex climbed back into the cockpit and smiled ruefully at David.

'You heard that?' she said.

'Yes. Looks like we get a night together after all!' His voice gave no indication of how he was feeling about that, in the light of his tacit decision not to prolong their relationship. Alex decided to treat the change of plan light-heartedly.

'Yes, and you'll be sleeping down in the dinghy unless you promise to behave.'

He assumed an injured expression. 'Me—misbehave? The thought never entered my head. I have been wondering, though, how we're supposed to get in behind the reef. I thought the idea was to stay away from them!'

'We'll manage,' she assured him.

They did, without too much difficulty, and David got

his extra sailing instruction in the process. It took an
hour or so to manoeuvre the boat into a good anchorage
and lash everything down. By the time that was done,
they were ready to eat again. Fortunately there was
plenty of food left over from lunch and a good supply of
drinking water.

Fortunately, too, the boat was a veritable home away
from home, with four bunks, complete kitchen facilities,
hot showers, even a stereo cassette player and a range of
tapes. A background of music helped the slight sense of
strain that descended when the time came to decide on
sleeping arrangements.

Alex hoped David would not be difficult when she
suggested that they use the rubber mattress from one of
the bunks to make up a bed for him on the dining table,
so that they had completely separate sleeping areas. He
accepted the arrangement nonchalantly enough, and
Alex was grateful. He agreed, too, that they share the
task of checking the anchor every two hours during the
night and volunteered for the first check.

Because their night would be disturbed by this task,
they decided to retire early. Alex always enjoyed going
to sleep to music, and tonight she felt it would help
alleviate the feeling of strangeness in their circumstances.
She consulted with David on choice of a tape and they
decided on Vivaldi's *Four Seasons*, as seeming somehow
appropriate.

She lay for a while listening to the music with its clear
notes of birds singing—the trilling of a goldfinch, the
repeated call of a cuckoo, the cooing of a turtle-dove, all
heralding an approaching storm, while outside the wind
could be heard in the trees not so far away on the island.
The boat rocked gently. Alex slept.

She woke with a start, to hear David moving about on

the deck overhead, and, with no idea what time it was, or whether she had slept through her turn to check the anchor, she rolled off her bunk and staggered to the foot of the ladder. Before she could begin to climb it, David began clanking down. She waited for him. He had a large torch in one hand.

'Everything OK?' she asked.

'All shipshape! I'm sorry I disturbed you. You *were* asleep?'

'Very soundly.'

She gained the impression that he had not been to sleep. She herself was wide awake now, and conscious that the earlier aura of constraint was still present, although it had a different quality now—it was an awareness of one another, that seemed to be drawing them together rather than isolating them.

'Well, goodnight again!' she said, and turned to go. But David's hand on her arm restrained her.

'Alex!'

He laid the torch on the table, then turned her so that she faced him, looking up at him questioningly.

'Yes?'

The indirect light from the torch gave an eerie glow and created strange shadows around them.

'You're so beautiful,' he murmured. 'I'd decided to go back home without saying anything, but I know I'll regret it for the rest of my life if I don't put up a fight for you.'

He drew her towards him, and she did not resist. In this isolated spot, with the wind raging outside and the boat rocking more strongly beneath them now, she was conscious of a primeval urge to seek something more than male companionship.

Perhaps the urge was stronger because, all day, she

had been nursing a deep sense of disappointment and resentment that Michael had made no effort to stop her going off for the day with David. He just hadn't seemed to care, as though it no longer mattered to him what she did or whom she saw. And there was his too-ready suggestion that they should not tell anyone that they knew one another. Alex had welcomed that at first. But now she wondered what really lay behind it—what his motive really was. And the fact that he had made no attempt to see her in the week since he had come to Mackay.

And here was David. So close, so kind, so understanding, so. . .*nice*. Why shouldn't she. . .?

She had allowed herself to remain quietly within his embrace while these thoughts passed through her mind. But when she felt his arms tighten around her and the steady beat of his heart beneath her ear quicken, she raised her face to his, to see what was there. . .

But his mouth found hers and he was no longer quietly comforting, but passionate and demanding.

She responded eagerly, her arms reaching up to encircle his neck, her body straining against his. But when she felt him stoop to lift her, her moment of madness ended. She recognised her response for what it had been and knew that there was nothing in it for David. It had been wholly selfish, based on her own needs. For his sake, she couldn't allow things to go any further.

'No, no, David! We mustn't!'

She pulled away and when his arms, reluctantly, released her, she moved back to lean against the table, feeling weak and breathless.

'Why not?' he demanded hoarsely. 'You said you're going to divorce Michael. I'll wait for you. I'll take you back to England with me. I'll make it up to you for all you've been through.'

She knew he meant what he said. But he had not said he loved her—and she could not say she loved him.

'No!' she said. 'This——' she waved a hand in a vague, inclusive gesture'—this is just. . .proximity. If we made love it would be for all the wrong reasons.'

'But you. . .'

'I know. . . I responded. I'm sorry, I shouldn't have. Please, David, let's just leave it!'

He looked at her for long moments, as if seeking for something in her face that would belie her words. Not finding it, he shook his head slightly, then said, 'If that's how you want it. . .'

'It really is!'

'Then I suggest you go back to bed.'

It was an abrupt dismissal, and she knew she had earned his anger. She turned and went, to lie on her bunk but not to sleep. She knew that he was not sleeping either, but when she took her turn to check the anchor he did not speak and she was glad.

She felt utterly miserable and alone. She could see only the one thing in her future—divorce. She realised that, when she had talked of divorce to David, it was the first time she had actually spoken the word in relation to herself and Michael. She had thought about it, of course, but it made it seem so much more real and imminent to talk about it.

Divorce! It was a horrible thing—something that happened to other people. She had never imagined that she, Alexandra McLachlan, would ever have a close encounter with it.

Towards morning, she realised that the wind had died

down and the boat was barely moving. And that she was hungry!

As soon as it began to get light, she went up on deck, and within a minute or two David joined her. He seemed relaxed and friendly and she took her cue from him and said nothing about the events of the night.

'Hungry?' she asked lightly.

'Starving!'

'So am I. And there's nothing we can do about it until we reach Airlie.'

'Then let's get moving!'

Alex knew that breakfast was not his only reason for not delaying.

She radioed the base and got the all-clear to come on in. 'Pick up buoy number twenty-three and we'll have a tender out to you in double-quick time.'

'Thank you, base.'

They made it back in excellent time, with a favourable wind, and the Whitsunday Charter people lost no time in putting them ashore.

Breakfast, in Airlie Beach, had never tasted so good, and then David took the wheel for the drive back to Mackay. He remained courteous and friendly. But he did not waste any time on the way and he was quite impersonal. Alex had a sense of anticlimax.

It was just nine o'clock when he stopped the car at the gate leading to the staff quarters of the hospital.

'Well, this is goodbye. I hope to arrange a flight out today, or tomorrow at the latest. Thank you for yesterday. It was most enjoyable.'

The night might never have happened.

'Thank *you*. I enjoyed it too,' Alex replied evenly.

His eyes held hers for a long moment and seemed to be saying all the things he had not, that morning. Then, as though his resolution had faltered, he leaned across and kissed her—tenderly, lingeringly.

As he straightened up, he realised that a car was passing, driving slowly, and that the driver of the car was looking at them, closely. David recognised the driver. Alex, with her back to the road, did not see the car and, by the time she turned round, it had disappeared through the hospital gates, fifty yards further up the road. She *did* notice that David had an odd expression on his face, and thought he was regretting the impulse that had led to that last kiss.

He got out, walked around the car and opened the door for her. She asked, as she stepped out, 'Can I drive you to your hotel?'

'No. I'm happy to walk.'

'Then. . .goodbye. I hope you have a good flight home.'

'Thanks. And you. . .look after yourself. I hope things work out for you.'

She smiled tremulously. 'Goodbye,' she said again, then slipped behind the wheel and drove away without looking back.

CHAPTER SEVEN

'IS THAT the lot for this morning, Sister?' asked Michael, shaking drops of water from his hands and reaching for a towel.

'Just one more, Doctor. You've had a long session.'

Sister Mann, brisk, grey-haired and efficient, straightened the drapes on the couch in the examination cubicle, disposed of a used kidney dish and a wooden spatula and straightened several small bottles on the bench as she talked.

'He's a new patient and he refused to give me any particulars, so I couldn't make out a card for him.'

'He's not a drug rep?' Michael walked out into the consulting-room and sat down wearily behind the big mahogany table. Sister followed and stood on the other side of the table.

'No,' she said. 'I know all the reps. And anyway, he's not carrying a case. I had a feeling he wanted to see you personally, but when I suggested he phone you out of surgery hours he said no, he had to see you here and now.'

'Intriguing,' said Michael. 'Let's have him in and solve the mystery.' He thought he knew what to expect—some man with a personal problem he was embarrassed about. Consultations like that could be difficult and prolonged—the last thing he needed right now.

He really was feeling excessively fatigued. As Sister said, it had been a long morning. And a boring one. Just one patient after another with a string of minor complaints that demanded little more than cursory examinations and prescriptions. Nothing to take his mind off the frustration and anger he had been feeling ever since he had seen Ally kissing that bloke yesterday morning, in her car, in front of the hospital. At nine o'clock! And the man had been sitting in the driving seat, so it wasn't just a casual encounter. If it had been, Ally would have been driving. Then, a few minutes later, Mike, getting out of his car in the doctors' car park in the hospital grounds, had seen the man walking along the road, alone, in the direction of town. So the kiss had been a farewell one.

One didn't have to be Sherlock Holmes to put all that together. There was only one possible conclusion. Ally and the man had not only spent the day together sailing, they had also spent the night together. Every time Mike thought about that, and it was often, he felt as though someone had landed him a punch below the belt.

He repeatedly kicked himself that he hadn't accepted the invitation to go sailing with them when he'd met them in Shute Harbour. If he had, there would have been no shenanigans afterwards—he'd have seen to that! But he had been so sure that David what's-his-name had been just a casual tourist whom Ally had met by chance and who was no possible threat to Mike's hopes of a reconciliation with her. How stupidly naïve could you be?

And how could *she* do it? He felt physically sick at the mental image of her with. . .

The door to the consulting-room opened and Sister was saying, 'Doctor will see you now.'

Mike tried to jerk his mind back into proper channels

for this last consultation. He forced his features into a professional smile and looked up.

The smile vanished.

Standing in the doorway was the man he had just been thinking about—David Bartel, who stood between himself and Ally.

'You!' he exclaimed, in most unprofessional tones.

Sister shot a startled look at him and paused in the doorway. But the doctor was oblivious of her and she had no option but to close the door and return to her desk. But not to work. She sat tensely, straining to hear what was being said on the other side of the door. There had been such unconcealed venom in the doctor's voice when he had said, 'You!' like that, that she knew anything could happen in there, even violence. She was prepared to intervene if things reached that stage.

The menace in Mike's voice and the anger in his pale, taut face and blazing eyes halted David just inside the door.

Mike stood up, and as he did so his hand closed around a heavy glass paperweight lying on the table. He seemed quite capable of launching it at the man facing him across the room.

David's motive in coming to see Michael had been wholly altruistic. He knew Michael could well have misinterpreted the kiss he had seen yesterday morning and he had decided to explain the nature of his relationship with Alex, before he left for England later on today. After all, as Alex's husband, Michael Jones deserved to know the truth. Also David, having accepted, regretfully but with no real heartbreak, Alex's refusal to become intimately involved with him, did sincerely want her to find happiness. He had sensed that she really was in love

Discover
FREE BOOKS
&
FREE GIFTS
From Mills & Boon

As a special introduction to
Mills & Boon Romances we will send you:

14 FREE Mills & Boon Romances plus a FREE
TEDDY & MYSTERY GIFT when you return this card.

But first - just for fun - see if you can find and circle four
hidden words in the puzzle.

R	D	A	V	R	Y	B	X	N	M
O	O	F	T	N	C	A	S	P	Y
Z	D	M	N	B	U	L	T	R	S
R	T	N	A	N	E	F	T	A	T
D	H	I	A	N	V	K	D	M	E
N	W	L	K	H	C	O	W	S	R
O	C	O	M	U	T	E	D	D	Y
I	L	V	F	L	P	B	T	I	E
P	E	E	J	S	G	I	F	T	P
S	P	N	S	E	T	I	R	N	E

**The hidden
words are:**

ROMANCE
GIFT
MYSTERY
TEDDY

Now turn over to claim your
FREE BOOKS & GIFTS

Free Books Certificate

Yes Please send me FREE and without obligation 14 specially selected Mills & Boon Romances, together with my FREE teddy and mystery gift. Please also reserve a special Reader Service Subscription for me. If I decide to subscribe, I shall receive 14 superb Romances every month for just £20.30, post and packing FREE. If I decide not to subscribe I shall write to you within 10 days. The FREE books and Gifts will be mine to keep in any case. I understand that I am under no obligation whatsoever. I can cancel or suspend my subscription at any time simply by writing to you. I am over the age of 18.

1A1R

Mrs/Miss/Mr _____

Address _____

_____ Postcode _____

Signature _____

FREE TEDDY

MYSTERY GIFT

Reader Service
FREEPOST
P.O. Box 236
Croydon
Surrey CR9 9EL

NO
STAMP
NEEDED

with her husband and that her happiness lay in being
reconciled with him.

But seeing him as he was now, he was not so sure
about that. There could have been things in her marriage—such as violence?—which he had not begun to
suspect. Anyhow, he had come here with the intention
of saying certain things and he didn't plan to leave until
they were said.

'I thought I should tell you. . .' he began. But he got
no further.

Mike was in no mood to be told anything—least of all
this fellow's story of what had happened between him
and Ally.

And anyway, he realised suddenly, how did this David
know enough about Ally's affairs to come here to see
him? If she had kept to their agreement, he shouldn't
know that they were anything more than professional
acquaintances. She must have told him quite a lot about
herself. Mike's imagination ran riot, imagining the pillow
talk the two of them had engaged in.

If the fire needed fuel added to it, that did it.

'There's nothing I want to hear from you,' he ground
out between clenched jaws.

'Nevertheless,' David persisted, 'I think you should
listen. It might be good for you.'

So this guy, on the strength of a one-night stand with
Ally and a one-sided version—hers—of her marriage
problems, was about to tell him, Mike, what was good
for him!

Not on your sweet Nelly he wasn't!

Mike had been to hell and part-way back in the last
few months, wondering what he had done to deserve
Ally's desertion. He was not about to have
this. . .this. . .gigolo tell him what he should be doing.

And if Ally had anything to say to him, she could come and tell him herself, not send some mealy-mouthed middle-man with a Pommie accent to do her dirty work for her.

'Will you leave. . .now! And you can tell my wife. . .'

There was no mistaking the regret in David's voice as he said, 'I shan't be seeing your wife again.'

Well, that's something, thought Mike. It was satisfying, too, that his adversary was clearly suffering at the thought of not seeing Ally again.

'I'm glad to hear that,' Mike said tautly. 'But that's all I want to hear from you. You will oblige me by not prolonging this visit.'

'As you wish,' replied David. 'But I *will* say just this, before I go. If your attitude towards me is any indication of what Alex had to endure, I don't wonder that she found her marriage intolerable.'

He turned on his heel and walked out.

He had gone, but his last words hung in the air, as though written there by some giant finger of judgement.

'She found her marriage intolerable.'

All the fight went out of Mike. He sank into his chair and dropped his head into his hands.

He neither saw nor heard Sister Mann get up from her desk, walk to the door and look in. She stood there for some moments, undecided whether to speak to him. But then, with a look of compassion, she closed the door quietly, gathered up her handbag and went home.

Mike heard the outer door click shut and realised dimly that he was alone. He could not remember ever having cried in his life, but he wished he could do so now if it would relieve this leaden lump in his chest.

This morning he had been miserable enough at the

idea of Ally with another man. But this was infinitely worse.

All along, ever since Ally had left him, he had clung to the hope that her reason for doing so had been some misunderstanding which could be put right, or some problem which time would heal. If it was because he had been too wrapped up in his work and his studies, he would do something about that. He would take steps to organise his time better, so that they could do things together, go places, entertain occasionally. . .

Or, if she wanted more money, he would somehow manage that too. Get a loan, perhaps, so things would not be so tight until he was on his feet professionally and could give her everything she wanted—everything he wanted to be able to give her.

Everything she wanted? Could it be that she wanted to start a family? That would be difficult—for a few years, anyway. He didn't see how they could make do just on his meagre income as a resident doctor. But, if that was what she wanted, he would find a way.

He had been over and over the ground so many times. He had been so sure that it was only a matter of finding out what it was that had been making her unhappy, and then making whatever adjustments that were necessary to put things right. After that, everything would be fine. Because basic to everything was the fact that she loved him, as he loved her. That being so, nothing was impossible.

He had never doubted her love for him—as he had never doubted his love for her.

Until now!

David Bartel's words had shattered his dreams for ever. Ally had 'found her marriage intolerable'. She had told David Bartel that! That could only mean that, somewhere along the way, her love for him had died. Because nothing was intolerable if two people loved each other.

He knew she had loved him when she had married him. He could never have been mistaken about that, not remembering those first few wonderful months. No! If he was sure of anything in this life, he was sure that their love, then, had been the solid gold, twenty-four-carat type.

Along the way, something had happened to stop her loving him. And he had been too stupidly blind and blinkered to see it happening. Without him ever having been aware of it, her marriage had become intolerable to her. Could she have been actually physically repulsed by it?

A long shudder shook him and a sound like a muffled sob broke the silence of the room.

The sound seemed to bring him back to awareness of his surroundings. He raised his head. The hands of the clock on the wall had advanced a whole hour since Sister had shown that last 'patient' in.

He knew that Sister had gone. But Ellen would have been expecting him home to lunch before this. Being a doctor's wife, she would have assumed that he was out on a call. But he should phone her.

Dully, his hand reached for the phone and when she answered he made an effort to speak normally as he told her he would not be in at all. He gave no reason.

That meant he had an hour before he should do his hospital round. An hour to regain what mental and emotional equilibrium he could. He would do something, go somewhere, alone.

He stood up, picked up his bag and went out, moving and feeling like a man twice his age.

CHAPTER EIGHT

ALEX'S sense of loss that followed David's departure lasted somewhat less than a day. Which was confirmation, if she needed any, that she had done the right thing in not becoming more involved with him.

She told herself she should be equally decisive about her relationship with Michael. She should simply go ahead and institute divorce proceedings.

But when she began to think about that, she found that the issues, which had been so clear-cut, had become a little fuzzy about the edges. She couldn't work up the same conviction that her grounds for divorce were, after all, valid.

She searched out, from among her private papers, the note Leonie Tyson had written to Michael and read it again. It was word for word as she remembered it—the evidence as damning as ever. Then why didn't she feel the same resentment?

She decided, quite definitely, that she would talk to Michael, really have it out with him and hear it from his own lips. Then she would decide what step she must take next.

He had surgery listed for Tuesday morning—a minor procedure, but it was just before her lunch-break. Perhaps they could find somewhere private and talk then.

But, when Tuesday morning arrived, she found that, for some reason, he had arranged for one of the other surgeons in the practice to substitute for him. This was not unusual for minor procedures and probably only meant that Michael had been called out in the night or was tied up on an emergency in the wards. Alex casually mentioned his absence to the stand-in surgeon, but the answer she got told her nothing. The surgeon didn't seem quite sure himself why Michael had asked him to sub for him.

She checked the lists for the rest of the week. Michael had nothing scheduled for the next two days. But that didn't mean she wouldn't see him. Most of the surgeons treated the unit like a home away from home. They would hold impromptu conferences in the corridor or talk about cases over coffee in their sitting-room.

Or drop in to talk to the staff about a forthcoming operation. That seemed to be her best bet. Friday's operation was a cholecystectomy and it was most likely that Michael would want to make sure she knew his preferences with regard to things like needle styles and suture types and gauges.

But he didn't come near the unit for any reason.

Until Friday morning.

From the minute he walked into the scrub-room, Alex knew he was unhappy about something. And it soon became apparent to her that the 'something' was herself. He said hello to the scout nurse but completely ignored Alex. He talked to Doug Weston, who was assisting, as they scrubbed. He said, 'Thank you,' to the nurse who tied his gown, but when Alex moved across to pick up his gloves and hold them for him, as he had always required her to do, he gestured her aside and picked up the first glove himself.

This was not lost on the nurse who, behind his back, opened her eyes wide and raised her eyebrows at Alex. As the two girls walked through to the theatre, Alex murmured, 'On your toes, girls,' and a minute later saw the nurse pass the message to the sponge nurse, who nodded philosophically. If a surgeon chose to be shirty, that was his prerogative. Nurses just had to grin and bear it.

Doug Weston and the anaesthetist seemed to pick up the vibes quickly too, because there was none of the light-hearted chatter and badinage that usually took place as the patient was being prepped and draped, and which was very helpful in relieving pre-operation nerves and tension.

Alex was completely nonplussed. The last time she had seen Michael was at Shute Harbour, and he had seemed quite relaxed then. He'd even let her go off with David without seeming to mind—a fact that still hurt her when she thought about it. True, he *had* hinted that he was not prepared to carry on with the current situation for too much longer. But that didn't explain his behaviour this morning. Something must have happened in the five days since Shute Harbour.

The situation in theatre didn't improve. Before long it must have been clear to everyone that she was the particular object of his rancour.

The light was wrongly positioned, he said. Alex reached up to adjust it with the autoclaved handle cover—infinitesimally, because it looked perfectly OK to her and she had no idea which way he wanted it moved. That was still not right. She moved it back to where it had been originally, whereat Michael said testily, 'All right! Leave it! Leave it!'

It went on. And on.

The suction was too weak.

She'd clamped the needle-holder too near the suture.

He fastened two clamps on the cystic duct and artery and said, 'Scalpel!' impatiently, even as Alex was holding it towards him. He positioned the blade between the clamps but, before he had barely begun to apply it, he threw it on to the floor.

'That blasted thing wouldn't cut shoe leather!'

Alex handed him another, thanking her lucky stars that she had put an extra one on her instrument trolley.

That incident was too much for even Doug Weston. Alex could see that the unspoken thought in his mind, as in everyone else's, was 'Prima donna surgeon'. And nobody, even other surgeons, liked prima donnas in the operating-room. Enough was enough.

Ignoring Michael, although he continued to hold retractors, tie off bleeders when necessary, do everything that was required of him as assistant surgeon, he began chattering happily away, first to the anaesthetist about the result of a local football match. Then he turned to one of the nurses.

'Nurse Caxton, isn't it? I thought so—know that red hair anywhere. Did you enjoy the party last weekend? Sophie always does put on a good show.'

For a few moments he had the floor all to himself, but gradually the atmosphere thawed and everyone, realising what Doug was doing, joined in.

Everyone but Michael, that was.

Even he couldn't fail to get the message. He had been judged guilty of behaviour unbecoming and was being sent to Coventry!

Alex didn't know whether to cheer for Doug or weep for Michael. He *had* deserved it. But he would not have behaved like that if he had not had some very nasty demon tormenting him.

When the operation was complete, he threw off his gown, gloves and mask and departed, not waiting for the other doctors as usual.

Alex lay awake that night, wondering what it was all about and whether she should still try to talk to him—if not about their future, perhaps to try and find out what was wrong.

Next day she passed him in the corridor and looked at him hopefully, wondering whether things were back to normal. But he nodded without speaking. And his eyes, for the brief second they met hers, were cold and bleak.

On Monday, he came into her office to use her telephone. He perched on a corner of her desk while he made his call. Alex could have reached out a hand and touched him, but she concentrated assiduously on the paperwork she was doing.

Michael finished his conversation and replaced the receiver. When he did not stand up, she raised her eyes from her work and looked at him. He was sitting, gazing down at his hands and looking so thoroughly miserable that her heart went out to him. And *that*, she thought at once, was a complication she could do without—it was one thing to be angry with him, but quite another to feel sorry for him. Quickly she said the first thing that came into her head.

'Can I help?'

'I beg your pardon?'

He seemed almost startled by the sound of her voice, but there was no anger in his voice as he responded—just. . .nothing.

'Er. . .no, thanks. I was just checking that Simon knows about Mrs Dunn's history of drug sensitivity before he orders her pre-medication for tomorrow.'

That sort of help was not what Alex had had in mind, but she refrained from saying so.

She searched about in her mind for some harmless comment she could make to try and break the barrier between them. Michael had seemed quite happy that day they had met in Shute Harbour, so she asked, 'Did you enjoy your day in Shute Harbour?'

His head jerked round and he stared down at her, with a frown between his eyes.

'Yes, I did.' And he had, but only because he had been so happy to discover that that fellow she was with had meant nothing to her. What a fool he had been!

He got up from her desk, said an abrupt, 'Goodbye,' and left.

Alex remained where she was, gazing down at the sheets of paper in front of her but seeing only his troubled face. Why, oh, why did she have to feel sorry for him? Things were confused enough without that.

It was ridiculous! Really it was! Here she was planning to divorce a man and all she could think about was how she could help him over a bad patch! When things had been different between them, she would have known just how to go about that. It had never failed. But she no longer had the right now.

She covered her cheeks with her hands for a moment. Then, with a deep sigh, she stood up and went in to see how the nurses were getting on preparing the theatre for the next operation.

The nurses were talking and laughing as they worked, as they usually did. Alex told them, sharply, to forget their social life while they were on duty and concentrate on their job.

When she had gone, the two nurses looked at one another in amazement. They had never seen Sister McLachlan like that before. It was bad enough having to put up with Dr Jones and his moods these days, without Sister being ratty too. What was the place coming to? It had been such a happy place to work at first. But now. . .!

CHAPTER NINE

ALEX was off duty and had slept late.

She was still in her robe, eating a snack in the chalet pantry, when the phone in the sitting-room rang. She padded in bare feet down the passage to answer it.

'The director of nursing would like to speak to Sister McLachlan.'

'This is Sister McLachlan.'

'Hold on, Sister, please.'

There was a click and the DON was on the line. She wasted no time on preliminaries.

'Sister, could you come to my office at once, please?'

'Certainly. But I'm off duty,' Alex told her.

'I realise that.' The DON's tone was crisp. 'I wouldn't intrude on your days off if it weren't important.'

'I only meant that I'm not yet showered or dressed,' Alex explained.

'Come as soon as you can, then.'

It was an unusual summons. As Alex showered and dressed, she searched her mind for something amiss she might have done, or left undone. She could think of nothing, but, because of the apparent importance of the summons, decided to dress in uniform.

Ten minutes later she walked into Administration and was shown at once into the director's office.

Miss Travers said, 'Sit down, Sister. I won't waste words. We've had a request for emergency aid from one of the more remote offshore islands. A woman, a patient of Dr Evans, has had a fall and fractured a leg, probably

107

a tibia and fibula. She's seven months pregnant and has had some irregular contractions since the fall. Unfortunately, both rescue helicopters are involved in the search for the missing hikers.'

Alex nodded. Everybody knew about the group of teenagers who had been missing for three days in dense rain forest. They were ill-equipped and fears were being held for their survival.

'Consequently,' Miss Travers continued, 'we've decided to send a medical team across by fast catamaran, to assess the patient's condition and decide whether or not to bring her back here. The team will need to take any equipment which might conceivably be needed across with them. We're asking you to go because you're both a competent surgical nurse and a trained midwife. Are you happy to go?'

'Of course! Who else. . .?'

'Dr Jones, as Dr Evans's locum.'

Alex's immediate reaction was to remember some urgent reason why she could not, after all, be included in the team. But she could think of nothing plausible and asked, 'Does Dr Jones know I'm being asked?'

Miss Travers looked as though she was wondering what that had to do with anything, but she replied, 'No. He left the choice of a nurse to me.' Then she continued briskly, 'Doctor will bring whatever he'll need to reduce the fracture, including anaesthesia. Sister Owens in Maternity has begun to assemble equipment you'd need if the patient should happen to go into premature labour and you were not able to transfer her back here. Of course, we'll be in radio contact and if a helicopter becomes available it will be sent over.'

A quarter of an hour later, Alex was standing in the foyer, just inside the main entrance conferring with

Helen Owens from Maternity Wing, in case they had omitted anything which should be among the equipment that an orderly and the ambulance driver were loading into the ambulance. Alex had been back to her room, thrown some items into a large tote bag and changed into slim white trousers and a short-sleeved cheong-sam-type top, which she sometimes wore as an alternative uniform. She had brought with her a padded anorak. The sun was shining intermittently, but a strong wind was blowing. Some bad weather had been forecast and Alex could see a build-up of dark cloud away to the east.

When she saw Michael's car arrive, she involuntarily shrank back further into the foyer. He manoeuvred the car past the ambulance and into the area reserved for doctors' cars near the entrance. He alighted quickly, took a case and a tote bag from the luggage compartment and moved across to the ambulance. He was wearing light fawn trousers and a cream short-sleeved shirt. He and Miss Travers promptly became absorbed in a list he held in his hand. After a few minutes they both nodded and he folded the list and thrust it into a hip pocket.

Miss Travers said something to him and he turned his head sharply and peered in the direction of the foyer. He moved forward and the doors slid open. Miss Travers came too, and claimed Helen's attention, so that neither of them saw the meeting between Alex and Michael. His expression was almost comical as he looked first at her and then at the bag on the floor by her feet.

Alex gave an expressive shrug and a wry, almost apologetic smile, implying that the situation wasn't of her choosing and they had no alternative but to make the best of it.

Michael's face stayed tense for a moment, then relaxed into a grin.

'So the lot fell upon Jonah, eh?'

Relieved that he could joke about it, she smiled back.

'That sounds ominous!'

'Don't worry,' he said. 'If we run into a storm and have to lighten ship, I'll see they jettison the humidicrib first.'

'Thanks a lot,' she said drily. 'Actually, I think the storm is a distinct possibility.'

'I agree.'

It seemed he had decided to call a truce, at least for the duration of the exercise, and for that she returned thanks. Their day would probably be difficult enough, without him being in the mood he had for the past week.

The ambulance driver indicated they were ready to move off. Alex and Michael said goodbye, went out and climbed up in front for the three-kilometre drive to the harbour.

At the marina, the catamaran was having difficulty holding its position in the steadily growing swell which intermittently slammed it against the sides of the wharf. Further out, the sea was sprinkled with whitecaps.

Michael looked at Alex and grinned. 'Had breakfast?'

'Yes. And I plan not to lose it.'

'Good girl!'

When the boat was relatively stabilised, he helped with the transfer and stowing away securely of the load of equipment from the ambulance. Alex assisted where she could. When that was completed to their satisfaction, Michael, on board, held up a hand to steady Alex as she stepped down from the wharf on to the wet metal deck. At that precise moment the boat rolled slightly and, good sailor though she was, her foot slipped and she stumbled and fell into his arms.

When she thought about the incident afterwards, she

could not decide whether it was his doing, or hers, that she remained there, with his arms around her, for several moments longer than was necessary for her to regain her balance. But it was he who finally broke away. Still clasping her forearms, he drew back, saying, 'Hey! Whatever happened to your sea-legs?'

The tone of his voice was light but, glancing up, she saw that his face was tense and his eyes bleak. It was their first physical contact since the night of the hospital party, and obviously he had not enjoyed it. She would be very careful that there were no more close encounters of any kind on this expedition.

She replied, her voice as light as his, 'I'm sorry! I'm not usually so clumsy in a boat.'

'I know.'

Of course he knew! Those days they had spent together on a boat—lazy, wonderful, golden days, with the wind in their faces and the sun hot on their scantily clad bodies. . .

She took a seat under the spray-guard as the boat eased away from the wharf. Suddenly its powerful twin motors roared and it leaped forward, riding high. It was exhilarating, splendid! She longed to turn her head to see whether Michael was enjoying it as much as she was, but refrained. Much better to maintain a professional attitude towards one another.

After a time, she became aware that he was standing behind her. She looked up and asked, in a carefully guarded voice, 'How long before we arrive at the island?'

He flicked a wrist to look at his watch and she was appalled at what the sight of the muscles rippling in his forearm, beneath the firm skin, did to her. She could feel, as though she were touching it, the fine, soft dark hair. . . She almost reached out a hand. What was happening to her? It was almost as though she was falling in love with him all over again! As if once wasn't enough! She should have her head examined!

The boat rose up as it met a wave, then sank into a trough. Alex put out a hand and clutched the gunwale, hoping he hadn't seen what was in her eyes.

He had to raise his voice against the wind and the roar of the outboards. 'We should be there in about forty to fifty minutes, if the skipper's calculations are correct and the weather doesn't deteriorate any further.'

Yes, he was certainly enjoying himself. His face was alight and his eyes glowing. He was quite unconscious of her presence.

To bring him back to earth, she asked prosaically, 'What do you think we'll find when we get there?'

He looked at her as though he didn't know what she was talking about for a moment, then said, 'Of course— you're right. After all, this is all in the day's work.'

He sat down opposite her. She had to keep her eyes on his lips to make out what he was saying above the noise, but she allowed herself to think only about what he was saying.

'The patient is a Mrs Hendricks—primipara—aged twenty-six. She's now seven and a half months pregnant and, according to Charles's notes, has kept well throughout. She and her husband are developing the island as a tourist resort. She had a fall—climbing a ladder, would you believe, at seven and a half months?—and has fractured her left lower leg. The radio call for help also mentioned that she's having some abdominal pain. That could mean something or nothing.'

'Your first job will be the fracture?' queried Alex.

'Yes. And let's hope it won't be a complicated one, since we won't have X-ray facilities to help us.'

'What type of anaesthetic do you plan to use?'

'I've been thinking about that and have decided that an epidural will be best in the circumstances. Hang on!' Michael grabbed Alex's arm as the boat slammed down the face of a large swell, the spray streaming past the sides of the boat.

'I'm glad it didn't get this bad when we were bare-boating from Shute!' Alex remarked, catching her breath.

Michael said nothing, but let go of her arm.

Alex, sensing sudden tension in him and not knowing what had caused it, resolved, again, to avoid mentioning anything whatsoever of a personal nature.

'Is there electricity on the island?' she asked, brushing the spray from her hair.

'Yes—from a generator. That was one thing I asked about this morning—for humidicribs, for one thing.'

They continued to talk about what they might find on the island and what they would do in the event of certain contingencies. It was reassuring, facing a task with as many imponderables as this one had, to be working with a doctor who was as decisive as Michael. Alex knew that this inspired confidence in him with the staff back at the hospital and was as much a cause of his popularity as his easygoing manner. Until the change in that manner a week ago.

'Hey, Doc!' a voice called from the other side of the cockpit.

Michael and Alex turned their heads to see the pilot pointing to a tree-covered island whose features were becoming more discernible as they approached. Soon they could see, behind a stretch of white sand, several low buildings, some of them still under construction.

Behind the tiny settlement, closely timbered hills rose, dark green against an ominously dark sky.

Then they could make out two figures on the sand, waving to them.

Michael waved back and said drily, 'I hope that just means "Hello" and not, "For heaven's sake, hurry!"'

The pilot grunted agreement and pulled the cat into a rather unstable-looking jetty, that, even in these more protected waters, was taking a beating from the swell.

Michael helped Alex out, without mishap this time. The men on the beach were pleased to see the cavalry arrive but not able to tell them much about the present state of things up at the house. They were carpenters, they said, working on the new building.

Michael said, 'Right! We'll go see what's what. If you chaps are free, you could give Pete here a hand unloading the boat. If your union allows it?' They exchanged grins and set to work.

The sand was dry and loose, and Alex had difficulty keeping up with Michael as he ploughed his way purposefully up the beach. Then he turned, waiting for her, and held out a hand. She took it and allowed herself to be drawn along.

As they approached the main building, a man appeared in the doorway and raised a hand in greeting. He was young, sandy-haired and stocky, with eyes of an intense light blue. He held out a hand to Michael.

'Alf Hendricks. Glad to see you.'

That was probably the understatement of the year, thought Alex, and caught Michael's eye, sharing the thought.

Michael took Alf's hand and said, 'Mike Jones. And this is Alex. . . Sister McLachlan. How are things?'

'So-so.'

Alf turned and led the way into a huge empty room which was obviously destined to be a dining-room one day. Alf didn't stop to make explanations. He was a man of few words and a single purpose at the moment. They followed him down a hall and into a bedroom.

Alex's first impression was that they were still on the beach. The room was full of light from a huge picture window that opened on to a wide panorama of sand and sea. She could see the catamaran and three figures moving about it. White cane had been used for furniture, but sparsely, and there was just one painting, a large abstract, on the wall opposite the bed. The decorator had clearly intended to let the view from the window dominate the room, and had succeeded magnificently.

Through a door in a far corner, Alex glimpsed a gleaming en suite bathroom and thought ruefully that it wouldn't be so spit-spot by the time Michael had finished plastering his patient's leg.

Alf had moved directly to his wife's side and taken her hand in his.

'This is Diane,' he said simply.

Man of few words though he might be, his devotion to his wife shone through them.

Diane was a plump, pretty girl, well advanced in pregnancy. Her blue eyes were clouded with pain and anxiety. But her soft brown hair had been recently brushed and she wore fresh, light make-up—Alf's work, no doubt. And only he, under the circumstances, could have had the room as neat and tidy as a hospital ward awaiting doctors' rounds. Diane's injured leg had been immobilised between sandbags made from the legs of tights and filled with beach sand.

'Well done, mate!' said Michael to Alf, indicating the

sandbags. Then, cheerfully, 'Hello, Diane! I'm Mike and this is Alex. I guess you're not sorry to see us!'

Diane nodded with a tense smile and Michael went on, 'Now, the sooner we get this leg fixed the more comfortable you'll be. Alf, while I see what's what here, could you rustle up a cuppa for us all?'

'OK, Doc!' Alf, obviously relieved to hand over the reins to someone competent, hurried out.

Michael laid gentle hands on Diane's leg and Alex, to distract her from what Michael was doing, sat down by the bed and asked, 'How are you feeling otherwise, Diane?'

She noticed her flinch and thought it was because of Michael's probing, until Diane's hands went protectively to cover her abdomen, above the thin cotton T-shirt she was wearing.

'You're having contractions, are you?' asked Alex, matter-of-factly, so as not to alarm her.

Diane did not seem too sure how to reply, so Alex asked, 'How frequently are the pains coming?'

Diane flicked a glance at Michael, then looked back at Alex, before saying, 'They don't feel like contractions. The pain's sort of. . .there all the time.'

Alex did not allow the concern she felt at Diane's reply to show in her face. She moved her hand to feel Diane's pulse, which she counted for fifteen seconds by her watch, then said cheerfully, 'That's fine! Now I'll have a listen to the baby's heart too.'

By the time she had checked the baby's heart rate with a stethoscope Michael had completed his initial examination and straightened his back. He smiled at Diane. 'You could have done a lot worse, young lady. It's a clean break and shouldn't give us any problems.' He glanced through the window and added, 'While Alf's getting the tea, I think I'll go down and help to bring the gear up.'

'I'll come too,' said Alex.

She saw Michael about to protest, but managed to catch his eye behind Diane's back. 'Why not?' he said, and to Diane, 'While we're gone, Diane, why don't you try and have a little snooze if you can? I'll close this blind for you.'

Diane looked doubtful but replied obediently, 'I'll try.'

'We shan't be long.'

They did not discuss her condition until they were clear of the house. Then Alex had to raise her voice to make herself heard above the wind that was howling through the trees behind them. Ahead, the seas had risen even more. It was clear the storm was going to break very soon.

Alex said, 'Aren't you optimistic, expecting that poor girl to take a nap, under the circumstances?'

'Actually, I don't. That was just a ruse to give me an excuse to close the blinds. We don't want her lying there watching us carry the gear up—it'd scare the living daylights out of her. Though they do seem a sensible young couple,' Michael added.

Alex said, 'I hadn't thought of that. Well done, Doc!' Then she hurried on, 'I came with you so I could talk to you.' Her concern sounded in her voice, and Michael turned and looked at her.

'Go on!' he ordered sharply.

'She's in pain, but she's not having contractions. Her abdomen's tense all the time.'

He winced. 'Any visible haemorrhage?'

'No. But her pulse is rapid—a hundred and ten—and a bit thready.'

'Could be nerves. But with the rigid abdo we'll have to assume we're dealing with a concealed haemorrhage from a partially detached placenta. Result of the accident, of course.'

'That's what I thought,' Alex agreed.

'Then the sooner she's delivered, the better, both for her and the baby. A seven-and-a-half-month infant— well, it's viable, but I'm very glad we didn't have to jettison that humidicrib, after all.'

His smile didn't reach his eyes, which were very thoughtful.

'No chance of transferring her to the hospital?' Alex asked.

'In these conditions, and without a helicopter, none at all, I'm afraid. Even if the helicopter were here, I'd think twice about it.'

They had stopped short, while they talked, a little way from the catamaran. Now Michael began walking again, rapidly, calling out as he did so, 'OK, you blokes! Action stations stat. Let's get this stuff to the house as quickly as we can.' He picked up a small crate and handed it to one of the men. 'Go carefully with that. Carry it like this,' demonstrating. 'Alex, you take this.' He handed her his own doctor's bag and she picked up his tote bag and her own as well.

The first heavy drops of rain began to fall as they all struggled, laden, up the beach. Under Michael's supervision, they piled the equipment in the kitchen, to be transferred to Diane's room as it was required.

The men went off, Alf returned to the bedroom and Alex and Michael began to wash their hands at the kitchen sink.

Michael was quiet for a while, then he explained, 'I'm just re-thinking the epidural.'

'In view of the haemorrhage?'

'Yes. But I'm still inclined to think it's our best option—less traumatic for a premature infant. I'll start an intravenous before I give the epidural injection, to help guard against hypo-tension. You'll monitor the blood pressure?'

'Yes. Frequently.'

'We've got ephedrine, oxygen, endotracheal tube. . .' He was talking to himself now. 'Right, let's go!'

In the bedroom, Diane was wide-eyed and visibly more uncomfortable than she had been earlier. Again, her hands were guarding her abdomen.

Talking reassuringly, Michael set about a series of observations, then suggested to Alex that she take a specimen of blood. 'Just for routine testing,' he assured Diane.

Alex knew he wanted it for grouping and matching in case a transfusion became necessary. She procured her sample without difficulty and filled in a form for the pathology laboratory back on the mainland.

Michael nodded approval when he read the form, signed it, then added, in his doctor's scrawl, 'APH ARM COPTER ASAP'. He was telling them, back on the mainland, that their patient was having an antepartum haemorrhage, that he intended doing a surgical induction of labour and that they wanted a helicopter on the island as soon as possible.

As Alex went off, with the form in her hand, to find Alf, Michael called, 'We'll hang on to the cat.' She nodded.

The storm was raging in full force now, but Alf was sure his foreman could make it to the mainland in the motor boat.

'Just the sort of caper he revels in,' he said.

Alex stressed the need for speed and that the man should wait at the hospital for whatever they gave him to bring back to the island.

A few minutes later, back in Diane's room, Alex heard the roar of a boat's engine starting up, and saw, through the sheeting rain, the boat nose out into deep water, then its reassuring wake as it accelerated with a roar, westwards.

Alex was busy in the bathroom with buckets of water and plaster bandages, preparing for the plaster casting of Diane's leg, when Michael came in.

'The foetal heart's not good,' he said quietly.

Alex's heart sank, but it was only what she had expected.

'We'll get the IV in pronto,' Michael decided.

Alex nodded and followed him into the bedroom.

Listening as Michael, seated on the edge of the bed, explained to Diane about the injection he was going to give her in her back so she wouldn't feel any pain while he fixed her leg, Alex felt a mixture of pride and tenderness. She had always known he would be like this with patients—that this was why he endeared himself to so many of them. And it wasn't just bedside manner— he really cared.

Yes, of course, he was saying now, Alf could stay.

Alf did stay. It must have been an ordeal for him, but he was staedy as a rock while Michael put the IV in Diane's vein, prepared and injected the epidural analgesic, reduced the fracture and encased the limb in plaster, with Alex's assistance.

While Alex cleaned up he inevitable mess that went with plastering, Michael talked to Alf and Diane again, explaining that her fall had caused the placenta—the afterbirth—to start to come away from the wall of the uterus, causing a small haemorrhage. It was that which was giving her tummy pains, and it was important for both Diane and the baby that she be delivered as soon as possible.

As Diane listened, her lips trembled and she turned to Alf beseechingly. He put an arm round her, stroked her hair with his free hand and murmured, 'Don't worry, honey! I'll be right here.'

And he was, for the long afternoon that followed.

Fortunately, Diane went into labour quickly after the induction and then progressed rapidly.

Alex, while she constantly monitored Diane's blood pressure and the baby's heartbeat, found herself listening, praying, for the sound of a helicopter. It could be vital, to have it standing by, if Diane's bleeding became uncontrollable, or if the baby needed intensive neo-natal care following the birth.

But it wasn't needed.

At five o'clock, the baby was born. It was a tiny girl. But she was pale and limp and lifeless. Alex and Michael had known what to expect—for too long Alex had not been able to hear the foetal heartbeat at all.

Nevertheless, she worked desperately to revive the baby, even while knowing it was hopeless. Michael laboured as desperately to complete the third stage of labour and stem Diane's haemorrhage.

He was eventually successful. Alex was not.

Alf and Diane watched, mute and wide-eyed, aware that their baby had not made a sound and of Alex's attempts to resuscitate her. When, at last, Alex looked at Michael with the barest shake of her head, Alf and Diane didn't need to be told. Alf took his wife in his arms and they wept together.

Alex wiped the baby's tiny, beautiful face and wrapped

the little form in a cuddle rug. Holding it in her arms, she turned her back on the bed and stood gazing out of the window. Out there, the storm had passed and the sun had broken through the clouds. A few seagulls were squarking raucously on the wet sand. Life went on as normal. But life was cruel, unfair.

Knowing that Alf was doing more for Diane than anyone else could and that they were best left alone for the moment, Michael went into the bathroom and removed his gown and gloves, before coming back to stand beside Alex at the window. He reached a hand and it closed over hers where it held the child.

After a few moments during which neither spoke, he gently took the bundle from her and walked to the bedside, placing it in Alf's arms. He knew Alf and Diane needed to see their baby, to accept the fact of her loss and to begin the grieving process.

Michael returned to Alex's side and placed an arm round her shoulders.

Then, barely audible at first but growing louder, they could hear the chuff-chuff-chuff of a helicopter. It appeared in the western sky, grew larger, hovered and settled on the firm sand, not far from where the catamaran rocked gently by the jetty.

Two figures alighted from the helicopter and stood looking up at the house. Nobody down there knew what had happened. Michael said quickly, 'Are you OK now, sweetheart?' When Alex nodded, he went off, to intercept the men on their way to the house.

Sad though she was for Alf and Diane, Alex felt a ray of warmth creep into her heart. Michael had called her 'sweetheart'! He probably hadn't even known he had done so, with his mind on other things, but somehow it helped to fill an emptiness she had been feeling all day as she had watched the closeness between Alf and Diane and their dependence on one another.

Michael and Alex and the paramedic who had arrived in the helicopter conferred in the kitchen and decided not to transfer Diane to the mainland until the next day.

She was receiving the blood which the paramedic had brought with him. Her physical signs had stabilised and her colour was good. Michael was eager to find out how the fracture looked on X-ray, but he agreed with the others that her psychological well-being was of first importance at the moment and that to spend the night in her own home would be the best thing for her, before she must face the helicopter trip and the unfamiliar environment of the hospital.

Pete would take the catamaran back to the mainland and the paramedic would go with him. Alex made coffee for them before they left.

Accommodation had to be prepared for the three who were staying, Michael and herself and the helicopter pilot. The pilot insisted that he would be happy sleeping on the beach near his machine. He had a sleeping bag, the rain had passed and the sky was clear with stars beginning to appear. It wouldn't be the first time he had slept out with his machine, not by a long shot, he told them.

Alf showed Alex several bedrooms which were adequately furnished for an overnight stay, though they lacked curtains and carpets. She selected two which were as far apart as possible. Somehow, the thought of sleeping in a room too near Michael's was disturbing.

She looked at her bed longingly after she had made it up with the linen Alf had provided. It was queen-size and inviting, and she was beginning to feel she needed

nothing more than to lie down and sleep. But before she
could do that, everybody had to eat, and that seemed to
be up to her.

Michael was keeping an eye on Diane and Alf was
there too, so Alex went to the kitchen and began opening
cupboard doors to see what she could find to make a
meal. She was standing, gazing into the big refrigerator,
when she was overcome by a feeling of intense fatigue
and sadness. Without warning, tears began rolling down
her cheeks. She brushed them away as she heard someone approaching, but she did not turn round.

'What can I do to help, chef?' asked Michael's voice.

'Eat scrambled eggs without complaining,' she replied,
still fossicking in the fridge. Scrambled eggs were his
least favourite food.

She turned round and caught his grimace. But he said
cheerily, 'If that's what's in the larder, then that's what
we'll eat.'

'There's plenty of stuff in the larder,' Alex said. 'It's
my energy supplies that are running low.'

He was immediately sympathetic. 'And fair enough
too, after a day like you've just had. Scrambled eggs it
is! And I couldn't think of anything better for Diane.'

He opened a door or two, and said, 'Good—herbs!'
Then, with his head in the refrigerator, he added happily, 'Mmm. You fix the eggs, while I fry us some bacon
and organise a green salad.' He opened the door of the
freezer. 'Bread rolls! A minute or two in the microwave
for them, and we'll have a feast fit for royalty.'

During their brief married life Alex had usually
insisted on preparing the meals, to give Michael the time
he needed for either sleeping or reading. They had
seldom pottered around a kitchen together, as they were
doing now. It felt—nice. And it was good not to be alone

just now. She wondered whether he had guessed that she would be feeling low and that was why he'd come.

While he prepared and tossed a big bowl of salad, she set trays for Alf and Diane and laid three places at the kitchen table. Then, as Michael's bacon sizzled in the pan, sending out tempting aromas, she beat up her eggs, added grated cheese and chives and popped the mixture into the microwave.

Michael took trays in to Diane and Alf and said he would check on her drip at the same time. Then the three of them sat down to their meal. Michael and Tim soon began exchanging experiences, of life in the air and life on the water. Alex knew that Michael's sailing stories, although founded on fact, were highlighted by more than a touch of imagination, and suspected that Tim's were too. But she wasn't about to be critical. She knew what they were doing—trying to take her mind, as well as their own, off today's events, and she was grateful. And having Tim there prevented any feeling of constraint that might have arisen between herself and Michael now that they no longer had the demands of their work to occupy their minds.

But eventually Tim went off and Alex and Michael were left alone. There was a brief silence, then Michael sighed contentedly.

'That was good,' he said. 'Almost like. . .'

Alex cut him off quickly. There had been quite enough emotion already today. The last thing she wanted to hear now was anything that began with 'Remember when. . .?'

'It's the first time I've seen you eat scrambled eggs and enjoy them,' she said.

'You do realise that we didn't have any lunch?' he reminded her.

'Now that you mention it, I do.'

She stood up and began gathering up plates and carrying them to the dishwasher.

'How shall we divide the night duty?' she asked.

'I'll take care of that. You get as much sleep as you can.'

'Oh, no! I'll do my share,' she insisted.

Finally Michael agreed that she could take over at two a.m., by which time the intravenous would be out and two-hourly checks should suffice. Alf intended to stay with Diane all night, catnapping in a big armchair beside her. They could rely on him to call them if necessary.

Alex said, 'Then I think I'll get what sleep I can now.'

She showered in the new en-suite bathroom, then discovered that she had not packed a nightgown. No matter. She had her gown to slip on for her visits to Diane's room, and a cream silk and lace teddy seemed even better than a nightgown for the humid night that followed the storm.

Above her, as she lay on the bed, a ceiling fan rotated lazily and through the open window she could hear the restless whisper of ripples breaking on the beach. She reminded her subconscious time-clock that she needed to waken at two o'clock and drifted into sleep.

She awoke at five minutes to two, brushed her hair and teeth, donned her gown and slipped along the passage. There was no sound from Michael's room or light showing as she passed his door. He was so used to snatching sleep at odd hours that she had no doubt he was well away now.

Alf stood up as Alex entered Diane's room, nodded that all was well and quietly departed. Diane seemed to be asleep, and Alex went across to read what Michael had written on the chart which they had kept throughout the day. As she stood there, she heard Diane stir and went across to the bed.

'How are you feeling?' she asked softly.

'Not too bad, I guess.' But, even as she spoke, her eyes brimmed with tears and they began rolling down her cheeks. Alex took her hand silently, knowing that, even if she could find words to say, they would sound trite and inadequate. But her unspoken sympathy was all that was needed to make Diane break into great, heartrending sobs.

Alex sat down on the bed and carefully put her arms round the girl, making soothing noises but not trying to stop the flood of tears. Diane needed to cry. Alex suspected that she had been fighting against it as long as Alf was in the room.

'It's. . .it's all my fault. . .' sobbed Diane.

'It was no one's fault. It was an accident.'

'I shouldn't have done it. . . I shouldn't have climbed the ladder.'

'You weren't to know. You mustn't blame yourself,' said Alex gently.

The tears abated somewhat. 'I don't want Alf to see me like this.'

'Alf knows how you feel. He probably feels the same. He'd be the last to expect you to be Superwoman.'

Alex settled Diane back on her pillows. She found her a clean handkerchief and brought a cold, wet face-cloth and hand-towel from the bathroom. When Diane had wiped her face, Alex took her set of observations and entered them below Michael's on the chart.

'Would you like a hot drink to help you get back to sleep?' she asked.

Before Diane could reply there was a chink of china

outside the door and Alf appeared, carrying a tray on which were a steaming jug and three mugs.

He put the tray down, turned to Diane and immediately her hand went out to him. Alex said quietly, 'Not for me, thanks, Alf,' and slipped out of the room.

Back in her room, she sank down on the bed, feeling inexpressibly sad—for Diane, for herself, for all the people in the world who were hurting at this moment. Nurses were taught that they must not become too emotionally involved in their patients' problems, but it was a precept Alex had always had trouble with.

And, of course, it was after two in the morning—an hour when nadirs were prone to happen. Perhaps she should have accepted Alf's cup of hot chocolate. At least it would have dealt with the low blood sugar which was probably a factor in her depression.

Low blood sugar, sympathy for Diane, the early morning hour—she knew they were not the basic cause of her fit of the blues. She kept seeing Diane's hand going out to Alf and knew that their closeness had served to underline the emotional emptiness of her own existence, the emptiness which had made her life during the last four months barely endurable.

It was only when she heard a soft tapping on her door that she became aware that there were tears on her cheeks. She brushed her hands across them and went to open it, expecting to see Alf.

It was not Alf, but Michael, standing there. And in his eyes was the swift realisation that she had been crying.

It added to her misery to see that he was wearing his old dark blue shave-coat and that, as always, the collar was tucked in at the neck. He never could remember to straighten it. She reached out a hand, then drew it back, remembering, just in time, that she no longer had the right to make wifely gestures. Her throat tightened unbearably and hot tears welled again. She closed her lips firmly to stop them trembling. The sight of weeping females had always made Michael uncomfortable.

But there was no condemnation in his eyes now. Only compassion and understanding—and much, much more. He held out his arms, and Alex let her tears flow unchecked as she went into them.

He held her tightly, his free hand caressing her hair. Then he guided her gently into the room and closed the door softly, probably thinking of Diane and Alf a few rooms down the hall.

The muffled click of the latch seemed to change everything. Alone in the room, any pretext that they were professional colleagues, conferring about a case, evaporated. They were not even, any longer, the comforter and the comforted. They were husband and wife, alone together as they had not been for four months. Those months, with their disappointments and disillusionment, their bitterness and frustration, melted away as though they had never been. There was only the present. And her body melting against his and his mouth finding hers in a long, deeply satisfying kiss.

Neither took the initiative and neither resisted. They were not aware of clothes being shed, of finding their way to the bed. There was no sense of unfamiliarity, no shyness. They had done this before, so often, and it was as natural and inevitable as two streams flowing together. It was thirst being assuaged and hunger appeased.

It was total bliss.

Afterwards, they slept in each other's arms and woke to love again—as they had done in the past. But they did not then, as they had in the past, lie side by side talking.

There was so much that would ultimately have to be said, but now was not the time.

Finally Michael stirred, looked at his watch and said, 'Four o'clock. I'll go and check on Diane.' But he sounded as reluctant to break the spell as Alex was to have it broken.

She murmured sleepily, 'Must you?' and remembered that that was what she had always said when, after a night of loving, he would have to get up early and return to the hospital.

He was remembering too, because he leaned across and kissed her, but soothingly so as not to arouse desire again.

'I love you, sweetheart,' he said.

Alex knew that this time he was fully aware of calling her that, and that he meant every delicious word of it.

'Love you too,' she said, and lay watching as he dressed. At the door, he hesitated and turned to look back at her, but she laughed and waved him on his way.

Alone, she stretched sinuously, feeling utterly content. There was still an hour or two of darkness, but she didn't want to go to sleep again. She wanted to stay awake and savour this sense of being vitally, vibrantly alive once more.

Only Michael had ever had the power to make her feel like this—complete, fulfilled and. . .cherished. She supposed she had been reasonably happy with her life before she had met him. But she had not really been alive until then. And when she'd left him it was as if that vital, living part of her had died. From then on, she had gone through the motions of living as though she were some sort of mechanical contraption—a robot.

She had thought the fires had gone out for ever, but she knew now that they had only been damped down, banked up, waiting to burst into flame at the right moment, with the right person.

The right person! Michael! Only Michael! What sort of fool had she been to think she could rebuild a life without him? It was because she loved him so much that she had been so devastated to think of him with another woman.

Leonie Tyson. She could think about Leonie Tyson quite calmly now. Having realised that, she decided she didn't ever want to think about her again. She belonged to the past. The future belonged to them—to Alex and Michael.

Certainly they would still have to talk. They would talk about what had happened, laugh about it, and forget it. It was past. Tomorrow was the beginning of a new era.

Not tomorrow! Today!

It was almost five o'clock and the sky was already lightening with the approach of morning. She would check on Diane and then get an hour or two more sleep. She would need it, considering what the day ahead would bring.

Diane was sleeping soundly and Alf was asleep in his chair too. Alex didn't disturb them. She noted that Diane's colour was good and that the pulse in her neck was strong and regular.

Alex returned to her room. It was already warm, the beginning of a hot day. She slipped off her gown and lay down without even a sheet to cover her.

She woke to find the room filled with sunlight and Michael standing by her bed. He was dressed in a light blue, open-necked shirt and white shorts. His hair was still wet from his shower. He had a tray in his hands and

he was smiling down at her with a look in his eyes which
she could not possibly mistake.

'You always were beautiful in the morning, Princess,'
he said tenderly.

Alex flushed slightly and moved to pull up the sheet,
but he reached a hand and stopped her.

'Hey! This is *me*, Mike. Remember? Your husband?'

'I do seem to remember. . .something.'

He deposited his tray on the table beside the bed and
sat down on the bed, taking her in his arms.

Five minutes later, knowing that one of them had to
be practical, Alex disengaged herself from his caresses,
which were becoming ever more insistent, enough to be
able to look at her watch.

'Eight o'clock!' she exclaimed. 'Why didn't you wake
me? How is Diane?'

'Diane's OK. How are *you*?'

'Need you ask?'

He bent to kiss her again, but she pushed him away,
laughing. He picked up the tray and placed it across her
knees.

'Orange juice, toast, marmalade, coffee—which may
be a little cold by now.' Then he became serious.
'Sweetheart, we must talk.'

She nodded. 'I know.'

'And soon.'

'Yes.'

'Today is obviously going to be a bit crazy,' Michael
went on. 'We have to get Diane safely across to the
hospital and that leg X-rayed. Then I'll have to see
what's cropped up for me at the surgery. But just as
soon as possible we'll spend time together and sort things
out.'

'I'll be waiting,' Alex said softly.

He stooped and dropped a kiss on her hair. But, as he straightened again, his eyes were serious and there was a tightness about his mouth. 'There's something I've got to tell you. . .'

He looked as though, after all, he wanted to tell her whatever it was right now, without waiting. She interrupted him quickly.

'Not now—later. I must get dressed. There's a lot to be done—I have to see to Diane. And what's been decided about the. . .the baby?'

He accepted, without further comment, her postponement of his. . .what was it. . .a confession?

'Alf and I have talked about that,' he said. 'They want her buried here, on the island. Alf will come back after he's seen Diane settled into hospital and there'll be a simple ceremony. Now,' he continued briskly, his mind on his work again, 'I must go and radio the mainland and see that all systems are go for our return.'

'And I'll give Diane a bed-bath and get her dressed and ready.'

All through the busy day that followed, Alex managed to keep her mind on her work. But underneath was a deep-seated awareness that all was, once again, right with her world.

CHAPTER TEN

ALEX was so happy she felt she hardly needed a helicopter to transport her back to the mainland. She had her own cloud nine to waft her into a future that held everything her heart desired. And when her eyes met Michael's, as they did several times on the flight, she was fairly sure he was feeling much the same. But, sensitive to Diane and Alf's so recent tragedy, they did not allow their happiness to be apparent.

The sky above them was an intense, rain-washed blue. Below was a kaleidoscope of colour, ranging from vibrant blues to aquamarine and emerald and turquoise. Dark green, heavily wooded mountainous islands were fringed by patches of brilliant white sand and light green fringing coral reefs. There were coral cays and blue lagoons and tiny white sails and larger pleasure cruise boats. It was magical scenery. Some day, they must come back here and enjoy it at their leisure—perhaps on a second honeymoon?

At the helicopter base an ambulance was waiting to take them all to the hospital. When they arrived there, Alex and Michael and, of course, Alf, accompanied Diane's stretcher to the Women's Surgical Unit. Alex saw Diane settled into bed, unpacked her bag and talked to her while Michael, at the nurses' station, made a full report on Diane's history and present condition. Then he came back into Diane's room, squeezed her hand and said, 'I'll be seeing you later today, young lady. You too, Alf.'

Alex left with him and in the corridor he said softly, 'I'll be seeing *you* later too, young lady.' His eyes were saying all the things that he couldn't, here. As Sister saw them and came bustling in their direction, he raised his voice and said formally, 'Well, thank you for everything, Sister McLachlan. You were. . .magnificent.'

Only Alex could see the laughter deep in his eyes and she felt a flush tinge her cheeks. He turned away from her and said to Sister, 'It was quite an experience, Sister.' Then his eyes clouded and there was genuine sadness in his voice as he added, 'If only we could have saved the baby!'

'Would that have been possible if you'd been here, instead of on the island?' asked Sister.

'No. It would have made no difference at all. The damage was done with the fall.' He paused, then said briskly, 'Well, I must be away. I'll see Diane this evening—we'll have the X-ray report before then.'

'Yes. I'll phone through to radiology immediately and arrange it,' Sister said.

'Good!' Michael turned to Alex. 'Thanks again, for everything.'

'Thank *you*, Doctor.'

The two sisters watched him walk away. There was a lightness in his step, and only Alex knew what caused it. She herself was feeling so vibrantly alive she wondered how long it would be before someone remarked on the change in her.

Sister watched Michael until he disappeared round a corner. Then she said, 'The more I see of that young man, the more I like him, and his work. You'll have quite a story to tell, my dear, but I mustn't stay to hear it now. Duty calls, as usual.' She began to walk away, but turned to add, 'Oh, by the way, the DON would like to see you when you're free.'

'I'll go now,' said Alex.

Miss Travers was eager to hear all that she had to report about their experience on the island. Alex was with her for twenty minutes, telling her story and answering some probing questions. Before she left, Miss Travers informed her that the OR duty roster had been changed so she could have her two free days, starting tomorrow.

On her way to the chalet Alex detoured through OR. Fran too wanted to hear all about everything but was too busy to stop just then. Alex was thankful for that. Fran's questions were likely to be even more probing than Miss Travers's, although along a different line, and Alex preferred to say nothing about the change in her relationship with Michael until she had had her talk with him.

She expected he would call that evening, and she stayed in the sitting-room where she could be the first to answer the phone when it rang. It did ring several times, but the calls were all for other people. Alex tracked those people down or wrote messages for them. In between times, she read magazines, or talked to anyone who happened to drop in. They all wanted to hear about her trip to the island and were inclined to be envious of her.

As the evening wore on, she debated whether to call Michael herself, but decided against it. She was sure he would phone her if he was not too busy, and if he *was* busy he would not appreciate the interruption.

At ten o'clock she went to bed and put her light out immediately, in case Fran should drop in for a chat when she came off duty.

She must have fallen asleep at once. When she was

wakened by a tapping on her door and a voice calling, 'McLachlan! Telephone!' it was still only ten-thirty.

She leaped out of bed, grabbed her gown and put it on as she ran, barefoot, down the passage to the sitting-room.

'Hello!' She made no attempt to disguise the eagerness in her voice. But it was not Michael on the other end, but her mother, and her mother sounded distressed.

'Alex, dear! I'm sorry to have rung you so late at night.'

'Mother!' Alarm took the place of happiness. 'What is it?'

'It's Gran, dear. She's had a stroke.'

'Oh, no!' gasped Alex. 'How bad is it?'

'She's in hospital. It's serious enough, but the doctor says if she doesn't have another one in the next few days her outlook should be good. But the next two or three days are vital. As soon as she regained consciousness she asked for you. Could you posisbly come?'

'Of course! I'll be there just as soon as I can. As it happens, I've got the next two days off. But how are *you*?'

'I'm coping—just. It will be so good to have you here.' Her mother's voice was tremulous, near to tears.

'Don't worry, Mum—Gran will make it. I'll let you know as soon as I can arrange a flight. Give Gran my love. Which hospital is she in?'

'Toowoomba. I'm staying in a hotel near the hospital.' Her mother gave details. 'I'm so glad you can come, Alex,' she said again.

'Nothing would stop me! See you soon.'

Alex hung up, went back to her room and sat on her bed. Gran! Her Gran, who had always seemed so indstructible and ageless. Alex felt as though her world was shaking on its axis. Gran had to recover, she couldn't. . .die! Alex found herself praying, silently, desperately.

She moved restlessly round her room, wondering how to fill in the interminable hours between now and morning when she would be able to arrange for a seat on a plane to Brisbane. She had no idea what time flights left Mackay, nor how she would get from Brisbane to Toowoomba, a hundred or so kilometres inland. It would all take time—too much time!

Suddenly she knew what she would do. She would drive, starting just as soon as she had dressed and packed a bag. She wasn't quite sure how far it was to Toowoomba—her maps were in her car—but she guessed over a thousand kilometres if she bypassed Brisbane by branching off the Bruce Highway some distance south. Even allowing for time out for a catnap if she became sleepy, she would be with her mother and Gran hours before she could otherwise hope to be. And it would be a real advantage to have her car there. Her mother didn't drive. Her life had been so sheltered she had never had any need to learn.

It was just eleven-thirty and nobody was about when Alex stole out to her car. She had decided against leaving notes for anyone. She would ring Michael from some-where en route in the morning and not contact Miss Travers until she had seen Gran and knew what to expect.

She drove steadily, stopping once for petrol. At three a.m., fatigue, reaction and hunger overwhelmed her suddenly. She stopped at a roadhouse for coffee and a sandwich, then drove a little further to a rest area, curled up on the back seat and slept for two hours. She woke feeling refreshed. Soon after she was back on the road, day began to break and traffic increased.

At eight o'clock, she stopped in Gin Gin and put through her call to Michael. He answered sleepily, sounded happy to hear her, then disappointed to know she had left Mackay and upset when she explained the reason for her sudden departure.

'I'm very sorry about your gran, honey. Give her a big hug from me. How long do you think you'll be away?'

'I don't know—two weeks? Perhaps three?'

'Princess, that's for ever!' he protested.

'I know, but it can't be helped.'

'Let me know how things are,' he told her.

'Of course.'

'I love you, honey.'

'Love you too. Bye.'

Side by side in her mind, for the remainder of that sometimes gruelling journey were her anxiety for Gran, empathy for her mother, happiness that everything was going to be all right with Michael and frustration that the final reconciliation with him had had to be postponed indefinitely.

At two-fifteen that afternoon, she was knocking on the door of her mother's hotel room and being greeted with exclamations of surprise, and with tears, as she and her mother hugged one another.

Her mother was dressed, ready to go back to the hospital. She agreed, gladly, to wait while Alex showered and changed, and meanwhile filled Alex in on Gran's condition. She had regained consciousness twelve hours after the stroke, which the doctors said was a good sign. Alex agreed. She couldn't move her limbs on the left side of her body and was still confused and restless. The nursing staff at the hospital had been absolutely marvellous and were hopeful and reassuring about Gran's chances of recovery.

All of this was confirmed when Alex, with her mother, stood by Gran's bed a little later. Gran seemed to be asleep when they walked in, but she opened her eyes at the sound of their voices, and there was no mistaking the gladness in her eyes when she saw Alex. Alex squeezed her good hand, kissed her gently and told her the nurses said she was doing just fine and would be home before she knew it. When Gran dozed off again, Alex and her mother sat in big, comfortable armchairs in the room, talking quietly and watching the nurses as they attended to Gran. Alex had to agree with her mother that the nursing care was excellent.

Next morning she rang Miss Travers, who was sympathetic about Alex's grandmother but inclined to want a firm assurance that Alex would be returning to her duties within a certain time. Finally she agreed to grant her three weeks' compassionate leave. Before the conversation ended, she asked Alex, 'You do regard your appointment to the hospital as a long-term one, Sister?'

'Oh, yes! I always have!' Alex assured her.

'That's good! Some of the staff are already showing signs of being professional tourists. Incidentally, Dr Jones had nothing but praise, when I talked to him, of your efficiency and co-operation during the emergency call to the island.'

'Thank you for saying so,' said Alex. 'I'm sorry I've had to ask for leave so soon.'

'I understand. And I hope your grandmother makes a good recovery. Goodbye, Sister.'

★   ★   ★

From then on, the days fell into a pattern of sorts, with coming and going between the hospital and the hotel, sleeping, eating, encouraging her mother to go for walks, do a little shopping, watch some television. Before long, they were able to encourage Gran and support the therapists in their rehabilitation programme.

Several times Alex drove her mother out to Avonleigh where they stayed the night and returned the next day. There had been good rains across the Darling Downs tableland and the country was looking lush and beautiful. Gran's property, in the care of an elderly overseer who had been with Gran for many years and whom Alex had known from childhood, looked particularly prosperous.

During the first week Alex was in Toowoomba, she had two notes from Michael. He did not say much—he never had been a letter writer. But it was good to get them, and she replied at more length, avoiding anything of a personal nature and mainly giving details of her grandmother's progress. The second week, she had a quick scrawl from him, on a prescription form, saying 'Busy ++. Love you +++. See you soon. Mike.' The third week there was a note from Fran, saying the town was in the grip of a flu epidemic, so she assumed Michael was being kept too busy to write.

Alex wanted desperately to ring him, to have the assurance of his voice telling her what she wanted to hear. But she refrained and refused to admit how deeply she was disappointed—and worried. She reminded herself that she would be seeing him soon, and carried on being positive and cheerful for her mother and her grandmother.

On Tuesday of the third week, she wrote a brief note to him, and another to Miss Travers, saying she would be back on Sunday to commence work on Monday.

Her grandmother was making good progress and there was talk that she would soon be able to be transferred to a nursing home in Goondiwindi, which was near enough to Avonleigh for her daughter to visit her each day.

On Wednesday, Alex received unofficial confirmation of something she had suspected for over a week. She couldn't wait to tell her mother and grandmother her news, knowing they would be almost as overjoyed as she herself was, and that it would give them something to look forward to in the long months ahead, of Gran's slow and painful return to health.

She went to the hospital that afternoon. Her mother was already there. Alex bent and kissed her grandmother. 'How was your day, Gran dear?' she asked.

Gran smiled heroically and said, slowly and with some difficulty, 'Everyone says I'm doing well, and I'm trying to believe them.'

'They're right, you know!'

Gran nodded, but Alex could see that she was more than a little doubtful, and guessed that she, and probably her mother also, was fully aware of what lay ahead. She knew that what she had to tell them would make a tremendous difference to their outlook on the future.

When Gran said wistfully, 'I do wish you could stay on, dear. It's been so lovely, having you here,' Alex knew that the time had come to share her good news.

'I'll ring you often,' she promised. 'And I'll get to see you just as soon as I possibly can. And when I come, I may bring someone else with me.'

'Oh?' They were both trying to be enthusiastic, but Alex could see that they were feeling less than overjoyed by the prospect of some unknown guest to be entertained.

'A nursing friend?' asked her mother politely.

'Not exactly. How would you both like to see Michael?'

'Michael! Oh, Alex! Yes!'

'But how. . .? Have you been writing?'

'No. By the strangest chance in the world, he's been working in Mackay too.'

Without going into great depth, she told them enough to satisfy them that all was going to be well between her and Michael.

But that was not all. She beamed at them and said, 'I didn't say anything before because Michael and I haven't really sat down and talked things out yet. But don't worry,' she added, as she saw concern replace the smiles on their faces, 'everything's going to be just fine. You see, I've just discovered that, as far as anyone can tell. . . I'm pregnant.'

Her mother said, 'Oh, Alex!' again, ecstatically. There were tears on her grandmother's face, but they were tears of joy.

'So, darlings, you can see that Michael and I really are back together again—for good,' Alex smiled.

'That's better than all the doctors' medicine,' said Gran. She sounded a little tired, though, and Alex soon suggested to her mother that they go to the hospital cafeteria for a cup of coffee and leave Gran to rest. On their way out, Alex stopped to tell the nurse at the station that her grandmother had just had some exciting news and might need a little extra sedation.

Over coffee, she told her mother that she had decided to go home tomorrow morning, a day earlier than she had intended. Her mother understood. 'You can't wait to tell Michael. And I don't wonder.'

Alex gave a happy little nod. She realised how easily that word 'home' had slipped off her tongue and that 'home' wasn't Mackay or the hospital or the nurses' chalet, but Michael. Where he was, from now on, would be home. And soon they would be a family!

She went to the hospital again that evening and Gran, a little tired from the excitement and sleepy from the extra sedation, accepted calmly the news of Alex's early departure.

Alex left next morning, very satisfied with everything. She felt confident her news had made a very positive contribution towards her grandmother's recovery and that it would buoy her mother up too, in the long months ahead. And she was going home to Michael!

She had decided to take two days for the journey back, arriving in Mackay late on Friday. She would contact Michael early on Saturday and they would have all day, or whatever time he was free, to talk.

Her future was as bright as the Queensland sunshine.

Alex arrived back at the chalet at six o'clock on Friday evening.

In case Michael was free and wanted to see her immediately, she showered and changed before phoning him at Dr Evans's home. Mrs Evans answered the call and said formally, 'I'm sorry, Dr Jones is not available. Is it an emergency? May I take a message?'

'No. It's a personal call. Do you know when he'll be in?'

'Well. . .' Ellen Evans seemed to be considering what to say and, when she did continue, gave Alex the impression that she was not very confident she was saying the right thing. 'I don't expect him back for some time—quite late, really.'

'I see. Then he's not on duty tonight?'

'No.'

'Is he free tomorrow?' asked Alex.

'I'm not sure. . . May I tell him who's called?'

'No, it's all right, thank you—I'll contact him later. Goodnight.'

Alex replaced the receiver, then sat for several minutes with her hand resting on it, telling herself she was foolish to feel so disappointed. After all, Michael was not expecting her back in Mackay until Sunday.

There was a chatter of voices as several nurses walked in the front door. Alex, looking up, saw Fran among them and Fran, catching Alex's eye, detached herself from the group and came into the sitting-room.

'Hi! Good to see you back. But we didn't expect you yet.'

'No. I came a little early,' Alex explained.

'How's your grandmother?'

'Improving steadily, thanks.'

Fran looked at Alex's hand, still resting on the telephone and said, 'I'm sorry—you were about to make a call. I'll catch up with you later.'

She made to go, but Alex interrupted.

'No—I've made my call. I was just sitting here, cogitating.'

'And not looking particularly pleased!'

'As a matter of fact, I tried to phone Michael, but he's out,' said Alex.

Fran looked surprised, and Alex expected a pertinent question about what had changed in her relationship with Michael that she should be trying to contact him. But the question did not come, and she did not know whether to be glad or sorry. If Fran had pursued the subject of Michael with her usual eagerness, Alex might have been tempted to pour out her story—and once she started it would be hard to stop short of adding the *pièce de résistance* about her pregnancy, and Michael must be the first to know about that.

So she was relieved, really, when Fran plunged into an account of what had been happening during Alex's absence. Alex expected any minute to hear Michael's name brought into the recital, but it didn't happen. In fact, Fran seemed preoccupied—not her usual self. Alex thought she knew why—Fran was tired.

'Thanks for taking over in theatres while I was away, Fran,' she said. 'I was sorry to have to leave so suddenly. Are you worn out?'

'Not really. Your replacement was quite good. We had some busy patches, but time enough in between to catch up.'

'Has Michael been in much?'

'About as usual.'

Once again, Fran did not follow up on the opportunity to talk about Michael. Alex was puzzled. Something had changed here. A suspicion entered her head. Was it possible that Fran had used her absence to try and make ground with Michael? She dismissed the idea as preposterous—not to be entertained on either Michael or Fran's account. All the same, she was sure there was something Fran was not saying.

Suddenly she yawned, then apologised. 'I've been driving all day,' she explained. As well, she was finding that, even so early in her pregnancy, she was needing extra sleep.

Fran jumped up from the arm of the chair where she had been perched and said, 'Of course, you're tired. I mustn't keep you talking. We'll catch up later.'

She went off, and Alex was left with the feeling that she had been glad of the chance to escape. Alone again, Alex sat, trying to explain to herself why it was that she was feeling mystified and apprehensive. She was sure it was not just because she had been unable to talk to Michael tonight. She dismissed her fears as being unjustified and imaginative, and went to bed.

She awoke early next morning, feeling refreshed and energetic. Her weeks of idleness seemed to have replenished her stores of vitality. She would drive downtown, have breakfast somewhere and then go for a walk in Queens Park before ringing Michael. Her fears of the previous evening had quite evaporated. She dressed in a light yellow dress which suited both her mood and the beautiful day.

By driving into town instead of walking, she could detour past Dr Evans's house. Just the sight of Michael's car in the driveway would be reassuring.

His car was not in the driveway. At this hour that could only mean that he was out on a call and, therefore, on duty today. But even so, Alex was determined to make contact with him, and soon.

She parked her car in almost the identical spot she had that day she met David Bartel, and was smiling as she walked into the coffee lounge, remembering how he had rescued her from the parking inspector. The lounge was almost deserted. Two or three people were seated at tables and several waitresses were chattering behind the counter.

Alex moved further inside, to find a seat away from the door. In the dim lighting, she passed a couple seated in an alcove against the wall. They were deep in conversation, facing each other across the small table. So engrossed were they that it was only when Alex gave an involuntary gasp and retraced a step or two to stand beside their table that they looked up. Her own amazement was reflected in their faces.

Michael and Leonie Tyson!

For a moment they all looked at one another. Alex felt rooted to the spot, until Michael began to stand up and to speak. Then she turned on her heel, colliding with a waitress who had been following her to a table, and almost ran from the shop.

Outside, in the dazzling sunshine, she could not for a moment remember where she was. She stood, in a state of shock, in the middle of the pavement while pedestrians walked around her, casting curious glances at her. She was oblivious of everything except the urgent necessity to get away from this place. She was too numb to even remember why she had to do that—realisation would come later.

She heard Michael's voice calling her name and was galvanised into action. She ran to her car, unlocked the door, got behind the wheel and drove off, without looking back.

She drove blindly, not knowing or caring where she was going. After a while, she realised that she was on the road she and David had taken the day they went sailing, the road to Airlie Beach. Why not? Airlie Beach was a long way from Mackay, and that was all that mattered. Alex forced herself to think about her driving. She began timing herself between mileage posts, then doing complicated computations about litres per kilometre of petrol consumption. Anything to occupy her mind so that she needn't think about. . .

When she began to feel very tired she remembered that she had not had breakfast. She had been meticulous about regular meals since she had known she was pregnant. And she shouldn't be driving with low blood sugar. Low blood sugar! When had she last thought about that? The night on the island. The memory was agonising. When she saw a roadhouse, she pulled in and ordered coffee and a sandwich and talked for a few minutes to the girl who served her. But she could not have said later what they had talked about.

It was not yet ten o'clock when she arrived in Airlie Beach. The day stretched endlessly before her. Airlie was frenetic with tourists and traffic, and she drove on, following a road which led away from the water, and eventually found herself at a lookout, called Coral Point, high above the harbour.

The view was magnificent, enough to capture even Alex's abstracted attention. A morning haze still shimmered on the water and through it she counted at least a dozen islands. She had an almost unbearable desire—an escapist wish—to be out there on one of those islands, away from everything.

She allowed herself to face the fact that, for three weeks, she had been living in a fool's paradise. In her state of euphoria, she had been ready to forget the past, to forgive whatever there was to forgive and to start over. Now her world was in shards about her feet again, and all because of Leonie Tyson.

What was Leonie doing in Mackay? Had Michael known all along that she was coming? Was that what he had wanted to tell her, that morning on the island—that Leonie was coming?

Leonie Tyson!

Suddenly she had become the central figure in every scenario from the past that flashed through Alex's tortured mind.

Was she the reason Michael had suggested, so promptly, that he and Alex behave like strangers towards one another, after he appeared in Mackay and found

Alex there—to leave the way open for Leonie's appearance on the scene?

Was that why he had seemed so unconcerned about her spending the day with David? Because he really hadn't cared?

Leonie! Everywhere her thoughts turned they encountered Leonie!

If only she had thought of Leonie Tyson that night on the island! She would not, then, have let Michael make love to her. She corrected herself. She had not 'let him make love to her', any more than he had let her. It had just happened. She wondered whether Michael was regretting it as bitterly as she was regretting it now. No, he couldn't be. Because he didn't know about. . .

Suddenly Alex knew what she had to do. She had to confront him. Traumatic though it would be, she had to hear him spell out to her what Leonie Tyson meant to him. What that night on the island had meant to him. Then she would know, finally, whether there was anything left that was worth fighting for.

She turned on the ignition and drove slowly down the hill and back to Airlie Beach. There she stopped for a quick lunch and in not much more than an hour was walking in the front door of the chalet. And the first person she saw was Fran. Suddenly her conversation with Fran last night made sense. She grasped Fran's arm urgently, and pulled her into the sitting-room. Fortunately the room was empty.

Fran protested, 'Alex! I'm supposed to be on duty!'

'This won't take a minute. Have you seen Michael recently with a woman—or have there been rumours of him with one?'

'Yes.'

'What kind of woman?'

'Attractive blonde type.'

'How long has she been in Mackay?'

'A week—ten days perhaps. Is she. . .?' queried Fran.

'Leonie Tyson,' said Alex. 'Of course!'

Fran looked confused. 'What's going on?' she wanted to know.

'I don't know, but I'm about to find out.'

'Alex, I wish I could help. . .talk. . .listen, whatever. But I must fly. They just rang over to say there's a road accident on the way in.'

Alex nodded. 'Of course. I'll talk to you later.'

She walked out of the sitting-room behind Fran and was in time to see her stop short as she was confronted by Michael, who had his hand raised to ring the doorbell.

Fran cast a frantic, sympathetic look over her shoulder at Alex, and fled.

Alex moved outside, not looking at Michael, and led the way to a clump of shrubbery, where they could neither be seen nor overheard from the chalet. Then she turned and looked at him.

He was looking grim. 'Where have you been?' he demanded. 'I've been trying to reach you all morning. When you took off like that this morning I was afraid you were ill.'

'No, I wasn't ill,' she said.

'Is your grandmother worse?'

This was bizarre!

'Look,' she said, 'I've just got in. We can't talk here.'

'Where, then?'

Alex shrugged helplessly and said nothing. He went on, 'Will you come to the house? Ellen's out at a bridge afternoon. We'd be alone.'

'I'll be there in half an hour.'

She went to her room, freshened up, combed her hair

and composed herself as best she could. As she was about to close her door she turned back, rummaged in a drawer and popped into her handbag the note that Leonie Tyson had written. In precisely half an hour she was ringing the bell of the Evans's front door.

Michael was there almost before she had taken her hand off the bell push. He led her into the big front lounge-room, then turned to her and was about to take her in his arms. She pulled away disbelievingly, and saw his face fall. He motioned her to an armchair and when she had sat down asked, 'Would you like a drink?'

Alex shook her head. He poured himself a gin and tonic and sat down opposite her, saying, easily enough, 'Now, what's all this about? I think you owe me an explanation.'

'*I* owe *you* an explanation?' She made no effort to keep the astonishment out of her voice.

'Yes. Of your behaviour this morning. Why didn't you stop and speak to Leonie?'

Alex was dumbfounded. Did he really expect she would not mind seeing him with Leonie—that she would stop and greet her like an old friend?

Michael was talking still. 'When you behaved like that, and after those very impersonal letters you wrote while you were away, I've been wondering whether you regretted. . .what happened. . .on the island.' His face looked pale and drawn. Alex could not know that he was hearing again David Bartel's voice saying, 'She found her marriage intolerable.'

She could only think that their discussion was taking most unexpected directions. But she had come here to get things straight and she was determined to do just that. In her own way. She must not allow herself to be sidetracked into discussing that night on the island.

She ignored his last remark and asked, 'Did you know Leonie Tyson was coming to Mackay?'

He looked puzzled. 'I think she had mentioned the possibility of passing through Mackay on her way to Cairns on leave.'

Alex had the first inkling that she had been wildly astray in her assumptions, somewhere. But she couldn't turn back now. She had to know—not only what was between Michael and Leonie now, but what there had once been.

She plunged in, head first. 'I was upset at seeing you with Leonie Tyson this morning,' she said in a low voice.

'You were. . .what?' He was struggling to understand.

'I think I had a right to be upset. After everything.'

'After what?' he persisted.

She reached down for her handbag, opened it, extracted a piece of folded paper and handed it to him.

'After this,' she said.

He looked at her, put down his glass and took the paper from her hand. He read it through quickly, frowned and looked up at her.

'Where did you get this? And what's it got to do with anything?'

'You must know. . .it has a lot to do with everything,' Alex retorted.

He read the few lines again. This time, when he looked up at her, there was the dawning of understanding in his eyes. And of something else that made her quail.

'I want to hear from you, now, just exactly what you thought this. . .missive. . .meant.' His words were measured, precise and she knew that there was no point in being evasive.

'I thought. . . I think. . .it meant that you and Leonie Tyson were. . .seeing one another.'

'You thought we were having an affair?'

Alex nodded mutely.

Michael looked as though he could hardly believe what he'd heard.

'Am I to believe that on the strength of this. . .' he flicked the paper disdainfully, 'you walked out on me, without a word, without giving me a chance to explain or defend myself?'

She could only repeat, 'I was quite sure I knew what it meant. And there'd been other things—rumours.'

'Rumours? In a hospital? And a few lines on a scrap of paper which could have meant something or nothing—you threw away our marriage for *that*?'

She knew by the way he enunciated every word, so precisely, and by the line of pallor around his lips, that he was more angry than she had ever seen him. But he remained coldly calm, as though he was keeping himself in check until they had reached the bottom of things.

Alex wanted to cry out, to defend herself. It hadn't only been the note, or the rumours. It was everything. All the little things that had disappointed and disillusioned her in what she had expected to be a perfect marriage. She wanted to tell him that loneliness was not compensated for by an occasional night of love. She felt she *had* tried to understand his situation, the demands of his working schedule, the need to spend interminable hours over his books. But *she'd* had needs too—the need to talk to someone when she had problems, the need for companionship.

Before she could muster her thoughts and begin to explain, he stood up and began pacing about the room.

'Let me tell you what this incriminating piece of

evidence is all about.' He paused and looked down at the
piece of paper he was still holding. 'I lost a patient one
night, a little girl, after a long and desperate fight. It was
in Leonie's ward—she was on night duty. I'd been on
duty for thirty-six hours straight and was exhausted in
every way. Leonie kept me sane, propped me up, fed me
cups of coffee, reasoned with me that I'd done all I could
for the child, that her death wasn't my fault. One can
never quite dismiss that feeling of guilt—that perhaps if
one had done something differently. . .'

He paused, and Alex knew that he was reliving the
trauma of that night. She understood. And she knew,
with a sinking certainty, that she had totally misinterpreted Leonie's note. The 'last night' Leonie had mentioned had not been a night of illicit love, as she had
imagined. And Michael's feelings of guilt that Leonie
had referred to were far different from what Alex had
thought.

'Why didn't you tell me?' she asked, in a voice little
more than a whisper.

'Because, when I saw you next morning, all you could
think about was that the flat had been broken into. And
frankly, at that stage, I was desperately trying not to
think about the night before.'

'It was *that* night. . .?'

'Yes.'

They were both silent for several moments, Michael
remembering, Alex trying to readjust her ideas to the
story Michael had told.

Then she said tentatively, 'You and Leonie talked
about money that night?'

He looked as if he were trying to remember. 'Yes, we
did,' he said eventually. 'As part of my downer, I
bewailed my lot pretty generally, talked about getting

out of medicine and into something more lucrative—I couldn't see the remotest possibility of ever being able to set up in private practice. Anyway, what's that got to do with anything now?'

'Who did Leonie mean when she said "as rich as you know who"?'

Michael looked blank, studied the note again briefly, then said, shortly, 'I don't know. . . I really haven't the faintest idea. Does it matter?'

His confusion was so obviously genuine that Alex could say nothing. She could only sit there, appalled at her own stupidity.

Michael appeared to interpret her silence as meaning that she was still waiting for an explanation, and went on impatiently, 'I suppose she meant Ben Cassidy. Wasn't he always supposed to be the richest man in the hospital?'

'Then why didn't she say Ben Cassidy?'

'Probably because she never could remember names of people. Hell! Does it matter?'

It was as though he could no longer hold himself in check. The storm broke and raged around her, and Alex knew she deserved every cruel word he flung at her. He talked a lot about love, but the word that recurred most often was 'trust'.

When, finally, he stopped and sank into a chair, dropping his head into his hands, she said, almost inaudibly, 'I'm sorry. I didn't know.'

'No, you didn't know! And you didn't care enough to find out the truth—just seized on the flimsiest of excuses to leave me. That says quite a lot about what our marriage meant to you. I've told myself over and over again that you must have had a good reason for leaving— that one day I'd discover what it was. If it was because

I'd neglected you, I'd have made amends. We could have started over. . .'

'We still can,' Alex interrupted urgently. 'I'm truly sorry. I made a mistake, a terrible one—I know that. But next time, I'd. . .'

'There won't be a next time,' he said harshly. With a quick, angry movement, he screwed up the note which he had held throughout, and flung it from him. 'If *that's* an indication of your love for me, of your trust in me, then I don't want anything more to do with you!'

She knew he meant every word he said. A feeling of hopelessness engulfed her. And, in that moment, she knew how much she had been counting on an ultimate reconciliation with him.

He was right, of course. Her love and her trust had been woefully lacking. What he did not know, and what she could never make him understand now, was that she was a different person from the one who had walked away from him four months ago. She felt infinitely older, infinitely wiser. She had grown up—she had needed to. She recognised how immature she had been. She had romanticised her marriage, had expected it to be perfect, more than human. She had been disappointed because he hadn't been perfect, and so she had been too ready to believe the worst of him. And now she would never have the chance to prove how much she had matured—how much she loved him.

He stood up and took a deep breath.

'Well,' he said, 'that's the end of that!'

And he meant it. He had just closed the book on that part of his life which had included her.

But, in her new-found maturity, Alex knew she couldn't leave without telling him all the truth. Not that she expected it to make any difference, but he had the right to know.

'Before I go, there's something I have to tell you,' she said quietly.

'Yes?' he said impatiently, as though he had no desire to prolong their meeting.

'I'm pregnant.'

'Pregnant?' Michael almost shouted the word. His face was white.

Alex said hastily, 'You must believe I'm not telling you this to make you change your mind about. . .anything. It's just that I thought you ought to know.'

He looked at her for a long moment before saying bitterly, 'And you expect me to believe that I'm the father of your child?'

She was astounded, disbelieving her ears. How could he say such a thing?

'Of course!' she countered. 'Who else. . .?'

'For all I know, it could be any one of a number of people. Your friend David Bartel, for instance?'

'David Bartel?'

'You can't deny you spent a night with him!'

She couldn't deny it. 'How did you know that?' she asked.

'I happened to see you early next morning—kissing him—it was most touching. And of course he came to see me that day, to tell me all about it, in case I hadn't got the message for myself.'

'David told you that. . .he and I ?'

'Actually, not in as many words—he didn't have to.'

'I can see it's no use trying to convince you that nothing happened between us?'

'None at all!' grated Michael.

'And *you* have the gall to talk to *me* about trust!'

Alex knew if she stayed here a moment longer she would burst into a furious, frustrated storm of tears, and what she might say to him would make what he had said to her seem mild by comparison.

She snatched her bag from the floor, stood up without looking at him again and departed.

The tears had to come. She drove to a remote, secluded part of the foreshore and, sitting in her car, facing the ocean, she cried until she was completely exhausted. Then, in a state of fragile calm, she reviewed her situation. There was no hope of a reconciliation with Michael—not after the things they had said to one another.

She forced herself to admit that, because of her foolishness, she had destroyed something that could never be rebuilt. For that, she had a sense of irreparable loss, as if she were grieving for the death of someone close to her. Worse than that! She felt as if she personally were responsible for the death.

But as, after a death, one had to go on living, so she would have to adjust her life and her circumstances and start again. After all, she was really only back to where she had been on the night of the hospital dinner, before Michael had appeared. But the raising of her hopes since the night on the island only made their demise so much harder to bear.

That night on the island! She hugged to herself the knowledge that she would have something to show for her marriage—her child, a child who had been conceived in love. Michael had still loved her then. It was only today, with the discovery of how she had failed him, that his love had died.

Realising that he had gone on loving her all those months, she faced, for the first time, what he must have endured in that time—wondering why she had left him. She had assumed that his guilty conscience would have told him why. But there had been no reason for him to have a guilty conscience.

When he had seen David Bartel kissing her that morning after their return from Shute Harbour, he had still loved her. No wonder he had been so bad-tempered in the week following that!

Her heart contracted with pity for him.

After a time, she forced herself to stop dwelling on what had been once, and what might have been, if only. . .and to face the future. Because of that one night on the island, it was not only her future, it was that of her child also.

She must leave the hospital before anyone knew she was pregnant. She couldn't face the curiosity, the wondering, the questions. She knew what she would do— she would go and live with her mother and grandmother at Avonleigh. Her baby would be born and grow up in the place she had always loved.

She wanted desperately to go back to the hospital, pack her bags and escape to Avonleigh now, without seeing anyone. But she couldn't do that. Bad news at this stage could jeopardise her grandmother's recovery. Every week that Alex deferred telling her that she wasn't, after all, reconciled with Michael would be better for Gran. Also, she had assured Miss Travers that she would not be leaving in the near future. The least she could do was stay as long as possible and then give adequate notice.

The tide was far out and the shadows were lengthening

across the wide stretch of sand below her car before Alex felt composed enough to return to the hospital and face people there. Nobody, least of all Fran, must suspect how drastically her life had changed in the last twelve hours.

CHAPTER ELEVEN

MICHAEL'S term as locum in Mackay would end in three weeks. Alex alternately dreaded and longed for the day when he would leave. She felt just as ambivalent about encountering him in OR, wanting to see him, yet dreading their first meeting since the final breakdown of their relationship.

His first case after her return to duty was listed for Tuesday. She felt literally sick as she dressed and went on duty that morning, and suspected it was a combination of nerves and morning sickness.

As soon as the night sister had handed over and departed, Alex made a cup of coffee with lashings of sugar and nibbled two cracker biscuits as she prepared the paperwork for the morning's list. That helped somewhat, but she was still on tenterhooks that, when Michael came, he would be as ill-humoured as he had been the week following David's departure.

She took good care not to be alone when he arrived. He greeted all the staff collectively and, apart from being a little pale and somewhat tense, was so nearly his normal self that Alex was sure nobody but herself would notice anything amiss.

He spoke to her no differently than he did to anyone else, and she was gradually able to relax and work opposite him with their usual rhythm and efficiency.

On Thursday, it was much the same.

On Friday, word flew round the hospital grapevine that Dr Jones had invited a nurse, Fiona Haigh from

Men's Surgical, to dinner and a dance the next night. Fiona was a petite, pretty blonde who laughed a lot. That was probably what had attracted Michael to her. Alex felt wildly jealous when she heard about it, then told herself she was being irrational and was glad Michael was not sitting home, alone, brooding.

On Monday he came into OR in such high good humour that one of the nurses felt bold enough to ask him cheekily, 'Had a good weekend, Doctor?'

He replied, 'Yes, you could say that,' and looked as though he meant it. Alex turned away and became very busy threading needles until she felt she could meet his gaze again without betraying what she was feeling.

She had several opportunities to go out herself in the next week or so, and was quick to seize them. Each time it was with a group, once to a movie, once to a restaurant. Another day they flew by amphibian to Hardy Lagoon on the outer Great Barrier Reef, and spent hours exploring the Reef, on foot, by glass-bottom boat and by snorkelling.

Fran too had become involved with her own circle of friends. Because Alex and Fran worked opposite shifts and never had the same days off, they did not see as much of one another off duty as they might otherwise have done. This was a relief to Alex now.

Fran did express concern a couple of times that Alex was quieter than usual, but accepted without question that it was because Alex was still concerned about her grandmother.

Towards the end of the second week, Alex was alone in the Unit, the other girls having gone to lunch at the end of that morning's cases, when Michael walked in.

She managed to conceal her surprise and a certain twinge of apprehension. She smiled up at him from her desk and, as he hesitated, looking around her office, she asked, 'Were you wanting something?'

'No,' he replied, then asked, 'How are you?'

'Fine. Why do you ask?'

'I thought you were looking a little peaky in theatre the other day.'

'Oh?' Alex was being purposely obtuse, giving nothing away.

'I've been thinking about things. Rather a lot, actually,' he said. 'I've come to tell you that I'll look after you and the. . .er. . .child.'

'Look after?' she echoed.

He made an impatient gesture. 'I mean I'll support you financially. At least until you can get back to work afterwards.'

'That's noble of you—seeing you don't believe the child is yours!' she said coldly.

He moved restlessly about the small room. 'I didn't say that, exactly. I suppose it could be mine. After all. . .you never really said you and. . .'

'David Bartel,' she supplied. 'No, I didn't, did I? But it seems to me it wouldn't make any difference to you and me anyway, now. That's not really the bottom line between us, is it?'

'No. I suppose not.' Michael picked up a pen, examined it searchingly, put it down again.

Alex said firmly, 'Thank you for your offer. It won't be necessary, however.'

'Nevertheless, I insist.'

'And I insist, once and for all, that I won't touch a cent of your money. So please don't bring the subject up again.'

She had spoken decisively, but he looked stubborn as

though he still wanted to argue. Alex got up out of her chair.

'Now, my nurses will be back any minute and I have things to do. If you'll excuse me.'

She pushed past him and walked out, leaving him standing there. It was a minute or two before she heard him walk out of the office and then the swing doors of the Unit open and shut.

So that was that! She wondered why she hadn't pleaded her innocence and told him that he was the only man who could possibly be the father of her child. She was glad she hadn't—it would only have made him the more insistent that he would support her and the child. The quicker and cleaner the break between them, the better.

There was another reason she had not declared herself innocent of an affair with David Bartel, but she could hardly have formulated it, even to herself. It had something to do with the guilt she felt for what she had done to Michael and the need to punish herself in an attempt to expiate that guilt.

Part of that guilt was for having suspected him of marrying her for her money. She hadn't thought about that for some time, but, if she *had* had any lingering doubts, they would have been dispelled now, with his offer of financial support for her, out of an income that was barely enough to support him, let alone provide for his future professional advancement.

Sudden tears burned her eyes and she scuttled quickly back into her office, sat down at her desk and bowed her head on her desk, feeling utterly miserable. She stayed thus until she heard the doors swing open again and the chatter of the nurses in the corridor. Then she stood up slowly, squared her shoulders and returned to work.

CHAPTER TWELVE

THAT night, there was a new and interesting subject for discussion in the sitting-room of the nurses' chalet.

Cynthia Jacobs, who worked in Women's Medical, had it from a patient who was a friend of Ellen Evans. Charles and Ellen were planning to take a party to Lindeman Island, as a special farewell for Michael at the end of his locum.

'A day trip?' asked someone.

'I rather gathered, a weekend,' said Cynthia.

'Who are the favoured ones?'

'That's what everyone's asking.'

'They'll probably be golfing friends of Dr Evans,' said one voice.

'Or bridge-playing friends of his wife,' put in another.

'Does Michael J play golf?'

Nobody seemed able to answer that, and Alex, who could have done so, was not about to.

The consensus of opinion was that, although everyone wanted to visit Lindeman Island, they would prefer to do it with a younger, brighter group than the Evanses were likely to muster. A pity, really, because Michael Jones was such a bright spark himself.

But they had done Charles and Ellen an injustice. The party that finally took shape was young enough, and bright enough, to cause considerable feelings of envy among those not invited. Fran Power and the nurse, Fiona Haigh, whom Michael had dated once, were among those who had received invitations. As well, there

166

were Walter and Jane Haysman, who were doctors in another practice and were young, attractive and fun-loving. The eighth was Doug Weston, and if he was a bit, well. . .naïve, it would do him the world of good to spend time with such a lively group.

When Fran heard that she had been included, she made an opportunity to talk to Alex, dropping over in her lunch hour and finding Alex in her room, writing to her mother.

Fran told her, somewhat tentatively, about her invitation and asked, 'Do you mind?'

'Why should I mind?' said Alex. 'I'm delighted for you.'

Fran looked at her keenly. 'I've been hoping you and Michael would sort things out while he was here. Has anything changed at all?'

'If you mean, are we any nearer to a reconciliation, the answer is a resounding no!' Alex's voice was a little louder than usual—that seemed the best way to keep it steady.

'It's a pity you had to be away for those three weeks,' said Fran. 'A little more time might have helped.'

'All the time in the world wouldn't have made any difference,' Alex said, unable, now, to keep the despond-ency out of her voice.

'Have you talked to him?' persisted Fran. 'I haven't liked to ask about the woman who was here. It *was* Leonie. . .?'

'Tyson. Yes. And yes, Michael and I have talked.'

'And?'

'And it's worse than ever it was.'

'So you were right in your suspicions about them?'

'No, I was completely wrong. There was never any-thing between them, except friendship.'

'Yet she came up here to see him while you were away.'

'She was passing through, on leave. She knew he was here, of course. *She* might have had other ideas, but as far as Michael goes I'm sure he was just being friendly in taking her round while she was here.'

Fran was looking mystified. 'But surely, if there's nothing going on between them and never has been, why can't you and he just make it up?'

Alex spread her hands in a hopeless little gesture. 'If you'd heard what Michael had to say about love and trust in marriage, you'd know there's no chance of that happening—ever!'

'Do you still love him?' asked Fran.

That was something Alex didn't want to admit, even to herself. She clamped her lips together to stop them trembling and gave an almost imperceptible nod.

Fran remained deep in thought for a minute or two. Then she stood up and squeezed Alex's shoulder sympathetically.

'Never say die, old thing. Love conquers, and all that. I know I'm an incurable romantic, but I'll keep hoping for a happy ending for you.'

'Happy endings are for movies. This is real life, and I'm learning the hard way that it's not the same thing at all.'

That was on Wednesday.

Thursday was a long, dreary day for Alex, with not enough work to take her mind off Michael's imminent departure. She wondered whether she would see him before he left. He had nothing scheduled in theatre for the rest of the week, but she knew he still had post-operative patients in the wards. Surely he wouldn't go without saying goodbye to her, if nothing more?

At ten-thirty that night she was propped up in bed with a book in front of her, but she was taking in very little of what she was reading. There was a knock on her door and Fran entered, still in uniform.

'Hi! I saw your light and dropped in to ask a favour of you.'

'Fire away!' said Alex.

'I'm suffering—really suffering—with the curse. Would you change times with me tomorrow so I can sleep in in the morning?'

'Of course!' Alex agreed promptly, then stopped. 'But tomorrow you're to leave for the weekend on Lindeman Island.'

'That's another thing! The way I'm likely to be for the next two days I'd be an utter wet blanket on a fun weekend. Could you possibly take my place?'

Alex frowned. 'But I'm on duty Saturday and Sunday.'

'And you're off on Monday and Tuesday, right? So we'll just swap days off and there we are.'

'But. . .don't you really think you can make it—dose yourself up with Panadol or something?'

'From past experience, nothing helps. Do, please, Alex, say you'll go!'

A fleeting suspicion crossed Alex's mind. This could be a ruse of Fran's to give Michael and herself one last chance at reconciliation. She looked hard at Fran. If she was putting on an act, she was doing it very convincingly, sitting on the end of Alex's bed, crouched over with her arms crossed across her tummy. And she did look pale.

The prospect that Fran's suggestion had opened up was like a shining vista of hope in a dark landscape for Alex. She wanted, quite desperately, to go. It might be disastrous, of course. Michael might react badly to her presence and spoil the weekend for everyone. He could ignore her for the two days. He might, even, simply refuse to go once he knew she was taking Fran's place.

That was a chance she had to take.

'If you're sure this is what you want. . .?' she asked Fran.

'Absolutely!'

'Then I'll do it.'

'Thanks, pal.' Fran jumped up off the bed with such alacrity that Alex's earlier suspicions were revived. She looked at Fran quizzically. 'I don't know that *I* shouldn't be thanking *you*,' she said drily.

'Not a bit of it! Just have a good time,' said Fran.

'I'll do my level best,' Alex promised her seriously.

'Attagirl! I'll ring Ellen Evans in the morning and explain things. And I'll see you before you go.' Fran went off happily.

Alex had very little sleep that night. Whatever Fran's motive had been for suggesting the change, Alex blessed her for the opportunity of seeing Michael before he left. Her thoughts were a confused mixture of anticipation and apprehension. The weekend could be a triumph, or it could be a disaster. But it could hardly make things worse than they were now. It could be that Michael would devote himself to Fiona Haigh and avoid Alex as much as possible. She knew that, in that case, she would inevitably find herself in the company of Doug Weston for much of the time. Ah, well! Doug had been with her when Michael had materialised in Mackay. He might as well be in at the end of the saga too. And he would be as unlikely, on the island, to notice if there were tensions and undercurrents present as he had been at the dinner dance.

At two a.m. Alex was still wide awake, so she got up and padded round her room, gathering things together, deciding which clothes she would take. She would need to talk to someone about transport arrangements. She did know that the plane left the airport for Lindeman Island at four-thirty, which would give her only an hour and a half between knocking off work and boarding the plane. In that time, she would have to shower, wash and blow-dry her hair, do last-minute packing. And she must make sure the DON approved the change of shifts.

Finally she slept.

On Friday, the hours flew by. At lunchtime, Alex ran across to the chalet to iron a frock she had decided to take for evenings. She found Fran in the pantry, deep in conversation with Fiona Haigh, and registered a fleeting impression that they seemed a little disconcerted by her unexpected appearance. But she snatched the chance to ask Fiona about transport to the airport. Fiona told her that Doug Weston was taking his car and would call for the two girls at the home at four-fifteen. Fran said she had been in touch with Ellen Evans. In Fiona's presence, Alex had to refrain from asking Fran whether Michael knew about the substitution of herself for Fran.

There were no hitches that afternoon. Doug Weston was on time and they arrived at the airport just behind Charles Evans's car. Alex could see Michael's head in the back seat and was conscious of a hard, nervous knot in her stomach. The two cars parked alongside one another and everyone emerged together. Alex avoided looking at Michael by continuing a conversation with Fiona while Doug Weston extracted their cases from the luggage compartment. Then greetings all round were inevitable. Michael gave nothing away as he said hello to her, and if he was a little quiet thereafter it was well covered by the chatter of the others as Walter and Jane

Haysman arrived. Charles and Walter both carried impressive-looking golf bags into the terminal.

As Alex had expected, Doug Weston managed to occupy the seat next to hers in the small plane. Charles and Ellen and Walter and Jane were seated in front of them, and Michael and Fiona were left to take the seats across the aisle from Doug and Alex. Alex and Fiona both had window seats, so Doug was between Alex and Michael.

The flight was smooth and took about half an hour, and the scenery below was breathtaking. Alex couldn't stop herself glancing across at Michael once, wondering whether he too was remembering their helicopter flight back from that other island when things had been so different between them. She found him looking at her, but she could read nothing in his face, and he looked away immediately and spoke to Fiona beside him.

The plane circled the island once before landing. Doug, who seemed to have done his homework, told Alex that Lindeman was one of the larger islands of the Whitsunday group. It consisted mainly of five hundred hectares of National Park. The first resort in the Whitsundays had been established there in the late 1920s.

Alex could see that there was a smaller island to the north of Lindeman and another to its south. Fringing coral reefs around the islands framed them in vivid green which merged into turquoise and sapphire and finally into deep endless blue. At intervals around the shoreline were stretches of brilliant white sand. The island itself was mostly covered in lush vegetation, and the Polynesian-style resort was tucked into a cove at its southern end. Alex glimpsed a large blue swimming pool surrounded by palm trees, set back from the dazzling wide white beach. There were tennis courts and a golf course which,

Doug informed her, was claimed to be the most beautiful in the world. On the water was a variety of craft, small sailing boats, catamarans, windsurfers, jet skiers. There would be no lack of something to do, if the company palled for any reason, thought Alex.

The north-south airstrip took them almost to the resort and they were soon being allotted rooms. All but the two married couples had single rooms, in double-storeyed buildings almost on the waterfront. It was arranged that they meet for dinner in one of the resort's two restaurants at eight o'clock.

Alex was glad of the opportunity to catnap on her bed for an hour or so. Now that the worst of her fears about Michael's reaction to her presence on the island had been allayed, she was feeling quite relaxed.

She dressed for dinner in one of her favourite outfits—vividly coloured, off-the-shoulder, slim-waisted, thinking it would not be long before her pregnancy meant a change of wardrobe. For now, she felt both refreshed and excited.

She was careful not to arrive early in the restaurant, in case she should find herself alone there with Michael. But her plan misfired. She arrived at the precise moment he did. He gave her a cursory glance, nodded briefly in greeting and said, 'We seem to be the last arrivals.' Then, placing a hand below her elbow, he guided her between tables to where the rest of the party were already seated. She could feel the hard muscles of his arm against her side and smell the subtle aroma of his aftershave. It was not one that brought back memories to her. She avoided looking at him until they reached the table, then, realising that the only two vacant seats were together, she glanced up at him, almost apologetically. He gave no hint that he was displeased at having to sit beside her during the meal. But he showed no pleasure either.

She forced herself to relax and greet the other members of the party with a smile. They all seemed to be watching her and Michael with more than casual interest, and she thought she sensed a slightly conspiratorial atmosphere. She wondered what they had all been talking about before she and Michael appeared. Whatever it was, Doug Weston, seated opposite Alex, was looking none too pleased.

Charles was seated on Alex's left and Jane on Michael's right. As if by common consent, Alex turned to talk to Charles and Michael to Jane as soon as they were seated. But the reprieve could only be temporary. Sooner or later, she and Michael would have to talk to one another, if people were not to notice that there was something unusual between them.

She recognised that that moment, when Michael turned to her, would be the first challenge of the weekend. She mustn't—she simply must not—blow it! Everything else could depend on establishing a relaxed, impersonal atmosphere at this stage. Above all, she must not make him feel threatened. If she could just manage that tonight, then, some time during the next two days, something might happen. . .she hardly knew what to hope for. . . She would play it by ear, take things as they came.

As she finished her entrée of prawn mousse in oyster sauce, she became aware that Michael had stopped talking with Jane and was sitting silently, as Jane turned to Doug, on her other side. Alex rounded off what she was saying to Charles and turned and smiled at the waitress who was removing her plate. She caught Michael's eye and said, 'That was delicious, wasn't it?'

'Yes. Seafood does seem the right thing to eat in a place like this.'

'It's all an unexpected treat for me,' said Alex. 'This time last night I was expecting to spend the weekend on duty in OR.'

'Oh?' he said politely, showing no great interest.

'Yes. Fran took sick at the last minute and insisted that I take her place.' Did she imagine a hint of scepticism in the slightly arched eyebrow with which he greeted this piece of information?

'I see,' he said, and added, 'Fran is a good friend of yours, I gather.'

Alex bit back the retort that rose to her lips at what he was implying and opted for a change of subject.

'Did you order trout for your next course?' she asked him.

'Yes. Fresh coral trout seemed too good to pass up.'

At that point, Charles leaned forward to ask Michael whether he had remembered to confirm his flight to Sydney, before leaving Mackay. Michael said yes, he had done that, and Alex asked smoothly, 'When do you leave, Doctor?'

Charles protested heartily, 'My dear, no formalities this weekend! Christian names only, please!'

Alex smiled and managed to maintain the smile as Michael replied to her question, 'I leave on Monday afternoon.'

So soon! She felt a sense of panic at the shortness of the time that was left to her.

Charles asked, 'Three-thirty, isn't it, Mike?' and Michael nodded, somewhat reluctantly, Alex thought.

From there, the conversation at their end of the table became general and before long the whole group were engaged in an exchange of medical anecdotes, which became more outrageous as the meal progressed, with Michael's contributions more so than the rest.

After dessert, Charles suggested that they drink their coffee on the terrace. As they moved out of the dining-room, Alex dropped behind Michael and began chatting with Fiona, but, after what seemed like some undue shuffling of chairs, she again found herself sitting beside Michael. She turned to him and said softly, 'I'm sorry. I tried not to. . .'

He looked at her coldly. 'If you want to move. . .?'

'Oh, no, I didn't mean that!' she protested. The fact that he made no effort to include her in the conversation convinced her that he thought she had manoeuvred to sit next to him. When someone suggested a disco, she got up quickly, said she was tired after working all day and wanted an early night. She said an all-inclusive goodnight and escaped to her room.

She really was tired. Even so early in her pregnancy, she seemed to need extra sleep and, of course, she had very little last night.

Her last thought before dropping off was that tomorrow she must avoid Michael as much as possible, in case he thought she was purposely seeking him out.

Unfortunately, when tomorrow came, that was not so easy to accomplish. In fact, it seemed almost impossible.

Charles and Walter went off early for a round of golf. By mid-morning, the others had emerged, one by one, from their rooms and gathered on the terrace by the pool. Someone suggested a short bush walk to a lookout on a hill, where there was said to be a most spectacular view over the islands. Ellen said lazily that she was too comfortable to move and would leave the climbing to the younger ones—they could take their cameras and bring her back some shots of the view. Just as the others were setting off, Jane decided to stay with Ellen. That left Doug and Fiona, Michael and Alex.

And that was how it stayed, on the narrow but well-defined path through the lush vegetation to the hilltop—Doug and Fiona went on ahead and Michael and Alex had perforce to follow. Michael looked at Alex with a nonchalant lift of the shoulders and a quizzical expression. Alex opened her mouth to speak, but he forestalled her. 'Please don't say you're sorry again.'

'Actually I was gong to ask, "Do you mind?"' she said with a small rueful laugh.

'There doesn't seem to be much we can do about it, except make the best of it. As far as I'm concerned, I intend to enjoy this weekend, whatever happens.'

The barb in his remark hurt her, but she ignored it and laughed suddenly. He looked at her with surprise and she explained, 'The grim determination in your voice when you said you were going to enjoy yourself struck me as funny.'

His face relaxed into a smile. 'Touché,' he said.

They walked for a while in silence, but it was not an awkward silence. They could hear Doug and Fiona chattering in front of them, as well as the chirping of lorikeets in the bushes all round them. The sun became warmer and the path steeper and Alex saw Doug reach out and grasp Fiona's hand. Michael said, 'Young love, do you think?' lightly enough, but there was a note of hard cynicism in his voice that hurt Alex. She reacted by asking, 'Do you mind?'

'Do I mind what?'

'You did date Fiona once or twice. I wondered. . .'

He made a dismissive gesture. 'Once only. And I don't think she enjoyed it any more than I did—which was my

fault entirely. I just wasn't my usual charming self.'
Again there was that bitter note in his voice.

They pressed on again in silence. The path became
even steeper and Michael turned to her suddenly, to ask,
'Should you be doing this?'

'I was beginning to wonder about that myself,' Alex
admitted. 'I didn't expect it to be such hard going.'

'Do you want to turn back?'

'No. We must be nearly there now.'

He held out a hand and, after a moment's hesitation,
she took it for the remainder of the climb, but dropped
it as soon as the ground levelled out at the top of the hill.

The panorama of sea, sky and islands was as magnificent as they had been led to expect, but Alex was too
conscious of Michael, standing very close to her in the
limited confines of the wooden lookout, to give it the
attention it deserved.

Doug and Fiona, clicking away happily with their
cameras, seemed not to notice the silence of their com-
panions. When their photographic zeal was exhausted,
they sank down on the wooden seats and everyone
chatted idly for a quarter of an hour or so, before taking
the path down again.

Michael held out a hand tentatively to Alex as they
started down the path again, but she gave a small shake
of her head and walked on ahead of him.

Lunch was a *smörgasbörd*. By the end of it, Alex was
positive that there was a plot afoot to get her and Michael
together, and that they were all involved in it.

Worse than that, as the afternoon went on, their
scheming became less and less subtle. There were sup-
pressed laughs and conspiratorial looks and one or two
suggestive comments. Michael could not possibly be as

unaware of it all as he appeared to be. Alex could only hope that he did not hold her responsible.

It was almost as though the whole situation was being taken out of her hands and she only had to allow herself to be carried along. She felt excitement stirring in her. It could, of course, be catastrophic. Or it could be the catalyst she needed to break down the barrier between herself and Michael, so that they could at least talk to one another.

The afternoon was hot and nobody ventured far from the pool. When the last rays of the sun were turning the sea to a riot of orange and red and gold, someone suggested a walk on the beach before dinner and they all bestirred themselves lazily.

The heat of the day had dissipated before a gentle breeze from the south. They walked in a straggling group to the farthest end of the beach, away from the resort, and sat down on the warm sand.

Behind them, a grove of palm trees rustled softly. The sea was dark now, with just a line of burnt orange on the horizon, broken by the silhouette of an island. The sky was a deep blue overhead and, as Alex watched, she saw the first star appear. She didn't have to think twice about the wish she would wish tonight.

Involuntarily, her eyes sought Michael's. He was watching her, and their gaze held for a long moment before she tore hers away.

Had he known—had he guessed—what she was thinking?

After a while she saw Charles and Ellen sauntering off back towards the resort. It was only when Michael spoke that she realised that the others had slipped away too, and that she and Michael were alone. He was sitting several feet away, but she feared that, even from there, he could hear the sudden thumping of her heart.

'Our friends seem to have deserted us,' he said. 'I suppose you realise what they're up to?'

Alex laughed, a trifle shakily. 'One would have to be thick as a plank not to!'

'I take it you're not. . .implicated?'

'Oh, no!' she protested. 'But I do have a suspicion about where it could have started.'

Fran's motive in asking her to take her place for the weekend was now definitely suspect. And she had enlisted Fiona to be her accomplice! Alex remembered how guilty Fran and Fiona had appeared when she'd interrupted their conversation in the pantry—was it only yesterday? And Fiona must have co-opted the others in the group. Doug had probably been the least willing of the conspirators. But, having realised that his chances with Alex were limited if there really was something going on between Michael and Alex, he seemed to have readily transferred his attention to Fiona.

So what had Fran told Fiona? Alex was confident she would not have betrayed her confidence to the extent of divulging that she and Michael were married. But she must have said enough to convince them that their efforts to promote a little romance on this tropical island were worthwhile, because everybody had played along with gusto.

Alex stood up abruptly and Michael followed suit.

'I think their games have gone on for long enough,' she said. 'I'm going back.'

He moved towards her and laid a hand on her arm.

'Wait!' he said. 'I want to know what you were thinking, a moment ago.'

'Only that it must have been Fran Power who put

them up to this. She's the only one who knows. . .anything.'

Her voice trailed away.

'*What* does she know?'

Alex turned her head away and her voice was so low that she thought he might not have heard her as she said, 'Only that I love you.'

She heard the quick intake of his breath before he said, almost as quietly, 'Shouldn't that be in the past tense?'

'No. Present tense.'

If there could be nothing else between them at this late stage, there could at least be truth.

Having committed herself so far, she knew she had to go all the way. She made no attempt to disguise what was in her heart as she looked at him and said, 'Could you. . .forgive me? Because I don't think I want to go on living without you.' Her voice faded into a sob.

'Oh, Ally!' He held out his arms and she went into them, as tears rained down her cheeks. 'Darling—don't! Please!'

Gently he lowered her until they were sitting on the sand. His hand was stroking her hair, his voice murmuring endearments. She wanted him to go on for ever. . .never to stop assuring her that he loved her. . .so much.

Then he was kissing her, and that was even better. And he did not stop for some time.

When he did, she said urgently, 'You do know, Michael, that there's never been anyone but you?'

'Deep down, I don't think I ever really doubted it. I was just mad with jealousy seeing you with that guy. And I was so hurt and bitter after you left me that I wanted to hurt you, the way you'd hurt me.'

'And I deserved it all! I was so stupid. But. . .' she drew a deep breath and said, with a touch of wonder in her voice '. . .do you know, I think I've really grown up at last. I had such childish ideas about marriage—wanting everything to be perfect. But I missed the most basic thing of all.'

'Which is?'

She smiled at him ruefully. 'Need you ask? Trust!'

Michael nodded. 'I did rather go on about it, didn't I? But I can't help feeling it's almost as important as love in a relationship.'

'Love is easy,' Alex said. 'I guess trust has to be learned.'

'I've learned a few things too,' he said. 'Perhaps it all had to happen. Just so long as it ended like this.'

He kissed her again, gently, lingeringly.

She gave a deep sigh of contentment. 'And now we're going to be a family!'

'Yes.' Michael was suddenly serious. 'You realise it won't be easy for a while, honey? But we'll manage.'

For a moment she was not sure what he was referring to. Then it occurred to her that she had another confession to make. She felt just a flutter of uncertainty about what his reaction would be.

'Michael. . .' She began.

'Yes?'

'There's something I haven't told you.'

'Oh?' He sounded unconcerned, as though nothing she could tell him would make any difference to the way he felt.

'We shan't have to worry about money any more.'

'Why not?' he asked.

'Because I have plenty.'

'You keep what you have, Princess. It's good to have

a nest-egg, for whatever. We'll manage.' He probably thought she had been saving her salary in the last few months.

'I mean. . . I really do have a lot of money. I always have had. . .' Her last few words faded away uncertainly.

'Always?' Michael was puzzled now, trying to understand.

'Always! My father left me. . .stacks really, when he died.'

He was silent for a long time, looking at her seriously, absorbing the implications of what she had said.

Then, 'I should have twigged when I saw Avonleigh. But if I thought about it at all, I guess I assumed that it all belonged to your grandmother. I don't think I ever, even subconsciously, related the obvious fact that the place smelled of wealth to you and me and our future.'

'And now?' Alex asked anxiously.

He was still looking at her, obviously fighting some battle with himself, and she held her breath, waiting for the outcome.

After what seemed an eternity, he said slowly, almost wonderingly, 'I guess I just did some growing up myself. All I know, Princess, is that nothing—absolutely nothing!—is going to come between us now. If that means living on my wife's money, well, so be it!' He chuckled. 'You never know—I might even come to like the idea!'

She gave a happy sigh and snuggled more deeply into his embrace. His arms tightened around her, in mute confirmation of his intention never to let her go. She raised her lips to his and they sealed their silent pact with a long, long kiss.

At length she stirred and murmured contentedly, 'Now I'm sure I've come home.'

'Sweetheart!' His soul was in his voice.

Alex sat up. 'When are we going to tell the others?'

Michael pondered for a moment, then his eyes glinted wickedly.

'We'll tell them all in good time. They've had their fun—now it's our turn!'

She eyed him doubtfully. 'I don't know that I trust you when you look like that.'

He said, with mock severity, 'Woman, will you never learn? I thought we'd resolved the question of trust once and for all.'

To which she replied, 'Sorry! I trust you absolutely.'

'Then just follow my lead.'

It was some time before she knew what he had in mind. They returned to their rooms. Alex showered and dressed and went to the dining-room. Michael was not yet there, but six pairs of eyes turned in her direction when she came in. She could read curiosity in them, and disappointment that she was alone. The same two seats were vacant. She took one of them, and a minute or two later Michael came in and sat down beside her. He was impeccably polite to her, as to everyone else, and Alex could feel everyone subside as their hopes died. Clearly their little ruse had not changed anything.

When the meal was finished, Michael smothered a yawn ostentatiously and said, 'Too much sea air, I guess. I'm for an early night.' He turned to Alex, held out a hand and said, 'Coming, darling?'

It was as unexpected to Alex as it was to everyone else, and the flush that flooded her cheeks had nothing to do with play-acting. Into the stunned silence that had greeted Michael's remark, he continued, addressing them all, 'We might have breakfast in our room in the morning. See you all at lunch. Goodnight.'

Alex mumbled, 'Goodnight,' and allowed herself to be led away. When they were out of earshot, Michael said, in injured tones, 'That wasn't very nice of them—not one of them said goodnight to us!'

'Michael, you wretch, how could you!' she protested.

They were outside now and in the shadow of the trees. She fell into his arms, laughing helplessly. He laughed too. 'Did you ever see such a group of stunned mullets? So much for the new morality!'

'Shouldn't we tell them?' asked Alex.

'We will—in good time. And, speaking of time, we're wasting precious moments. Let's go get your things from your room.' His voice softened as he said, 'Princess, this is going to be a night to remember, for both of us.'

It was.

There were no barriers now. No misunderstandings. No doubts or reservations. There was something in their lovemaking that had never been there before—some deep sense of fulfilment and of promise, of commitment.

Lunch next day was something that Alex would remember for a long time too.

They were all there when she and Michael arrived, hand in hand. Everybody tried very hard to behave normally, until Doug asked naïvely, 'Did you have a good night?' Then they all began talking at once to cover his gaffe.

Alex blushed furiously and looked at Michael appealingly. But he gave a tiny shake of the head and placed a restraining hand on her knee beneath the table. 'Not yet,' he whispered, so only she could hear.

Charles began heartily talking about the golf they had played that morning. Only Ellen was very quiet. Alex told herself that, if Michael did not tell them the truth very soon, she would do so herself.

Towards the end of lunch, Charles asked, 'What's everyone going to do this afternoon?'

There were several suggestions. It was a lovely day and they all opted for water sports. . .sailing, water-skiing, para-sailing. . .

Michael raised his voice to make sure they all heard him as he said to Alex, 'You'd better not do anything too strenuous, darling.' Then he turned to them all and explained, 'Alex is pregnant, you see.'

Alex gave a horrified gasp and jumped to her feet. Michael's little game had gone too far! She must intervene before he said something even more outrageous. But she couldn't make herself heard. After a pungent pause, everyone was talking at once. They all seemed to have decided that Michael, a renowned prankster, was having them on. If the truth were known, he and Alex had not spent the night together, after all. It was all part of the joke.

Charles, chuckling, said, 'Pull the other one, Mike!'

Walter said, 'Hey, mate, that's coming the raw prawn just a bit too thick. You'll be telling us next you carry a pregnancy testing kit around with you for just such emergencies!'

Michael just sat there, looking fatuous. Alex had had more than enough. She rapped a spoon loudly on the table to get everyone's attention. When they had quietened down somewhat, she explained, very earnestly, 'What Michael hasn't told you is that he and I are married.'

To her surprise, this didn't have the desired effect at all. They all fell about laughing once more. So Alex was a practical joker too, like Mike! The pair of them had probably worked all this out together, last night, to get even.

Walter said, 'I suppose you just happened to run into a marriage celebrant on the beach, and Mike said, "I do" and Alex said, "I will". Good try, Mike, but no dice!'

Alex looked helplessly at Michael. 'You explain—in a way they'll understand,' she begged. 'No more nonsense. . .ple-e-ase!'

He grinned. 'Words of one syllable, eh?'

He stood up. They all watched him, smiling, expecting more nonsense.

'Unaccustomed as I am to public speaking. . .'

'Hear, hear!'

He waited patiently, then went on, 'My wife and I. . .' He gazed down at Alex fondly. There were more catcalls and laughter, but he was not deterred. 'My wife and I wish to set the record straight. We really are married—have been so for roughly two years.'

There were some exclamations of disbelief, but they were watching him intently now, beginning to believe him.

'You see,' he went on, 'we've been separated for some time. It was quite by chance that we both turned up in Mackay. After some private discussions, we decided to keep our guilty secret and behave like strangers to one another, for the duration of my locum. Which we have done, with the exception of one notable. . .er. . . hiccough, some weeks ago! He looked down at Alex and grinned. She blushed.

Everyone nodded their heads knowingly, and said, 'Aha!' to one another, meaningfully.

Michael continued, 'Now, thanks to Providence and certain interfering friends who shall be nameless——' he included them all in a low bow '—our schemes have gang agley, and, as of last evening, Ally and I are fully and finally reconciled.'

It was the first time they had heard Michael call Alex by his own diminutive of her name. Somehow that clinched it. They *had* to believe him now. Even if they hadn't, the look he and Alex exchanged as he reached for her hand would have convinced them.

They were all talking at once, expressing their amazement, pleasure, congratulations. Ellen Evans was beaming widest of all.

Michael was completely serious as he said, 'Thank you, all of you, for your good wishes, for your friendship, and for your scheming little games. If it hadn't been for them, who knows. . .? Ally and I do plan to have a long and happy life together, but what's left of today we want to spend with all of you—with our friends. So, as Charles was saying earlier, what are we going to do with what's left of today?'

Charles was on his feet. 'Before we do anything, I think a toast is called for. Waiter!'

What remained of lunch became a celebration party. Toasts were drunk and speeches made.

Last of all, Alex had a toast of her own to propose.

'To an absent friend—Fran Powers.'

Michael raised his glass. 'To Fran! Bless her conniving little heart!'

But it wasn't Fran he was thinking of as he smiled down into Alex's eyes.

— MEDICAL ROMANCE —

The books for your enjoyment this month are:

EASTERN ADVENTURE Lisa Cooper
DANGEROUS PRACTICE Sheila Danton
ENTER DR JONES Judith Hunte
THE CURE FOR LONELINESS Jennifer Eden

Treats in store!

Watch next month for the following absorbing
stories:

A DREAM WORTH SHARING Hazel Fisher
GIVE BACK THE YEARS Elisabeth Scott
UNCERTAIN FUTURE Angela Devine
REPEAT PRESCRIPTION Sonia Deane

Available from Boots, Martins, John Menzies, W.H. Smith,
Woolworths and other paperback stockists.

Also available from Reader Service, P.O. Box 236,
Thornton Road, Croydon, Surrey CR9 3RU.

Readers in South Africa — write to:
Independent Book Services Pty, Postbag X3010,
Randburg, 2125, S. Africa.

A
SPECIAL GIFT
FOR
MOTHER'S DAY

Four new Romances by some of your favourite authors
have been selected as a special treat for Mother's Day.

**A CIVILISED
ARRANGEMENT**
Catherine George
THE GEMINI BRIDE
Sally Heywood
**AN IMPOSSIBLE
SITUATION**
Margaret Mayo
LIGHTNING'S LADY
Valerie Parv
Four charming love stories for
only £5.80, the perfect gift for
Mother's Day . . . or you can
even treat yourself.

**Look out for the special pack
from January 1991.**

4 MEDICAL ROMANCES
AND 2 FREE GIFTS
From Mills & Boon

Capture all the excitement, intrigue and emotion of the busy medical world by accepting four FREE Medical Romances, plus a FREE cuddly teddy and special mystery gift. Then if you choose, go on to enjoy 4 more exciting Medical Romances every month! Send the coupon below at once to:

MILLS & BOON READER SERVICE, FREEPOST PO BOX 236, CROYDON, SURREY CR9 9EL.
No stamp required

--- ✂ - ✂ ---

YES! Please rush me my 4 Free Medical Romances and 2 Free Gifts! Please also reserve me a Reader Service Subscription. If I decide to subscribe, I can look forward to receiving 4 Medical Romances every month for just £5.80 delivered direct to my door. Post and packing is free, and there's a free Mills & Boon Newsletter. If I choose not to subscribe I shall write to you within 10 days – I can keep the books and gifts whatever I decide. I can cancel or suspend my subscription at any time. I am over 18.

EP02D

Name (Mr/Mrs/Ms) _____

Address _____

_____

_____ Postcode _____

Signature _____

The door to her past awaited – dare she unlock its secrets?

AVAILABLE IN
FEBRUARY. PRICE £3.50

Adopted at sixteen, Julie Malone had no memory of her childhood. Now she discovers that her real identity is Suellen Deveraux – heiress to an enormous family fortune.

She stood to inherit millions, but there were too many unanswered questions – why couldn't she remember her life as Suellen? What had happened to make her flee her home?

As the pieces of the puzzle begin to fall into place, the accidents begin. Strange, eerie events, each more terrifying than the last. Someone is watching and waiting. Someone wants Suellen to disappear forever.

WORLDWIDE